The Manxman
Part II

by

Sir Hall Caine

Double 9 BOOKS

The Manxman Part II

by Sir Hall Caine

ISBN: 978-93-63055-00-1

Published by

DOUBLE 9 BOOKS

2/13-B, Ansari Road
Daryaganj, New Delhi – 110002
info@double9books.com
www.double9books.com
Tel. 011-40042856

ABOUT THE AUTHOR

Sir Thomas Henry Hall, better known as Hall Caine, was a British novelist, dramatist, short story writer, poet, and critic in the late nineteenth and early twentieth centuries. Caine enjoyed exceptional fame throughout his lifetime. He published fifteen novels on infidelity, divorce, domestic abuse, illegitimacy, infanticide, religious prejudice, and women's rights, becoming a worldwide literary celebrity and selling 10 million copies. Caine was the highest-paid novelist of his day. The Eternal City is the first novel to sell more than one million copies globally. Caine was born in Runcorn to a Manx father and a Cumbrian mother, but grew up in Liverpool. Caine received architectural draughtsman training after completing four years in school. He spent his boyhood holidays with family in the Isle of Man. At the age of seventeen, he spent a year as a schoolmaster in Maughold. After that, he returned to Liverpool and began a career in journalism, eventually becoming a leader writer for the Liverpool Mercury. As a lecturer and theatre critic, he formed a network of prominent literary contacts who impacted him. Caine traveled to London at Dante Gabriel Rossetti's recommendation and stayed with the poet, serving as secretary and companion throughout Rossetti's final years.

CONTENTS

PART II
BOY AND GIRL

I

Auntie Nan had grown uneasy because Philip was not yet started in life. During the spell of his partnership with Pete she had protested and he had coaxed, she had scolded and he had laughed. But when Pete was gone she remembered her old device, and began to play on Philip through the memory of his father.

One day the air was full of the sea freshness of a beautiful Manx November. Philip sniffed it from the porch after breakfast and then gathered up his tackle for cod.

"The boat again, Philip?" said Auntie Nan. "Then promise me to be back for tea."

Philip gave his promise and kept it. When he returned after his day's fishing the old lady was waiting for him in the little blue room which she called her own. The sweet place was more than usually dainty and comfortable that day. A bright fire was burning, and everything seemed to be arranged so carefully and nattily. The table was laid with cups and saucers, the kettle was singing on the jockey-bar, and Auntie Nan herself, in a cap of black lace and a dress of russet silk with flounces, was fluttering about with an odour of lavender and the light gaiety of a bird.

"Why, what's the meaning of this?" said Philip.

And the sweet old thing answered, half nervously, half jokingly, "You don't know? What a child it is, to be sure! So you don't remember what day it is?"

"What day? The fifth of Nov—oh, my birthday! I had clean forgotten it, Auntie."

"Yes, and you are one-and-twenty for tea-time. That's why I asked you to be home."

She poured out the tea, settled herself with her feet on the fender, allowed the cat to establish itself on her skirt, and then, with a nervous smile and a slight depression of the heart, she began on her task.

"How the years roll on, Philip! It's twenty years since I gave you my first birthday present I wasn't here when you were born, dear. Grandfather had forbidden me. Poor grandfather! But how I longed to come and wash, and dress, and nurse my boy's boy, and call myself an auntie aloud! Oh, dear me, the day I first saw you! Shall I ever forget it? Grandfather and I were at Cowley, the draper's, when a beautiful young person stepped in with a baby. A little too gay, poor thing, and that was how I knew her."

"My mother?"

"Yes, dear, and grandfather was standing with his back to the street. I grow hot to this day when I remember, but she didn't seem afraid. She nodded and smiled and lifted the muslin veil from the baby's face, and said 'Who's he like, Miss Christian?' It was wonderful. You were asleep, and it was the same for all the world as if your father had slept back to be a baby. I was trembling fit to drop and couldn't answer, and then your mother saw grandfather, and before I could stop her she had touched him on the shoulder. He stood with his bad ear towards us, and his sight was failing, too, but seeing the form of a lady beside him, he swept round, and bowed low, and smiled and raised his hat, as his way was with all women. Then your mother held the baby up and said quite gaily, 'Is it one of the Ballures he is, Dempster, or one of the Ballawhaines?' Dear heart when I think of it! Grandfather straightened himself up, turned about, and was out on the street in an instant."

"Poor father!" said Philip.

Auntie Nan's eyes brightened.

"I was going to tell you of your first birthday, dearest. Grandfather had gone then—poor grandfather!—and I had knitted you a little soft cap of white wool, with a tassel and a pink bow. Your mother's father was living still—Capt'n Billy, as they called him—and when I put the cap on your little head, he cried out, 'A sailor every inch of him!' And sure enough, though I had never thought it, a sailor's cap it was. And Capt'n Billy put you on his knee, and looked at you sideways, and slapped his thigh, and blew a cloud of smoke from his long pipe and cried again, 'This boy is for a sailor, I'm telling you.' You fell asleep in the old man's arms, and I carried you to your cot upstairs. Your father followed me into the bedroom, and your mother was there already dusting the big shells on the mantelpiece. Poor Tom! I see him yet. He dropped his long white hand over the cot-rail, pushed back the little cap and the yellow curls from your forehead, and said proudly, 'Ah, no, this head wasn't built for a sailor!' He meant no harm, but—Oh, dear, Oh, dear!—your mother heard him, and thought he was belittling her and hers. 'These qualities!' she cried, and slashed the duster and flounced out of the room, and one of the shells fell with a clank into the fender. Your father turned his face to the window. I could have cried for shame that he should be ashamed before me. But looking out on the sea,—the bay was very loud that day, I remember—he said in his deep voice, that was like a mellow bell, and trembled ratherly, 'It's not for nothing, Nannie, that the child has the forehead of Napoleon. Only let God spare him and he'll be something some day, when his father, with his broken heart and his broken brain, is dead and gone, and the daisies cover him.'"

Auntie Nan carried her point. That night Philip laid up his boat for the winter, and next morning he set his face towards Ballawhaine with the object of enlisting Uncle Peter's help in starting upon the profession of the law. Auntie Nan went with him. She had urged him to the step by the twofold plea that the Ballawhaine was his only male relative of mature years, and that he had lately sent his own son Ross to study for the bar in England.

Both were nervous and uncertain on the way down; Auntie Nan talked incessantly from under her poke-bonnet, thinking to keep up Philip's courage. But when they came to the big gate and looked up at the turrets through the trees, her memory went back with deep tenderness to the days when the house had been her home, and she began to cry in silence. Philip himself was not unmoved. This had been the birthplace and birthright of his father.

The English footman, in buff and scarlet, ushered them into the drawing-room with the formality proper to strangers.

To their surprise they found Ross there. He was sitting at the piano strumming a music-hall ditty. As the door opened be shuffled to his feet, shook hands distantly with Auntie Nan, and nodded his head to Philip.

The young man was by this time a sapling well fed from the old tree. Taller than his father by many inches, broader, heavier, and larger in all ways, with the slow eyes of a seal and something of a seal's face as well. But with his father's sprawling legs and his father's levity and irony of manner and of voice—a Manxman disguised out of all recognition of race, and apeing the fashionable follies of the hour in London.

Auntie Nan settled her umbrella, smoothed her gloves and her white front hair, and inquired meekly if he was well.

"Not very fit," he drawled; "shouldn't be here if I were. But father worried my life out until I came back to recruit."

"Perhaps," said Auntie Nan, looking simple and sympathetic, "perhaps you've been longing for home. It must be a great trial to a young man to live in London for the first time. That's where a young woman has the advantage—she needn't leave home, at all events. Then your lodgings, perhaps they are not in the best part either."

"I used to have chambers in an Inn of Court——"

Auntie Nan looked concerned. "I don't think I should like Philip to live long at an inn," she said.

"But now I'm in rooms in the Hay market."

Auntie Nan looked relieved.

"That must be better," she said. "Noisy in the mornings, perhaps, but your evenings will be quiet for study, I should think."

"Precisely," said Boss, with a snigger, touching the piano again, and Philip, sitting near the door, felt the palm of his hand itch for the whole breadth of his cousin's cheek.

Uncle Peter came in hurriedly, with short, nervous steps. His hair as well as his eyebrows was now white, his eye was hollow, his cheeks were thin, his mouth was restless, and he had lost some of his upper teeth, he coughed frequently, he was shabbily dressed, and had the look of a dying man.

"Ah! it's you, Anne! and Philip, too. Good morning, Philip. Give the piano a rest, Ross—that's a good lad. Well, Miss Christian, well!"

"Philip came of age yesterday, Peter," said Auntie Nan in a timid voice.

"Indeed!" said the Ballawhaine, "then Ross is twenty next month. A little more than a year and a month between them."

He scrutinised the old lady's face for a moment without speaking, and then said, "Well?"

"He would like to go to London to study for the bar," faltered Auntie Nan.

"Why not the church at home?"

"The church would have been my own choice, Peter, but his father——"

The Ballawhaine crossed his leg over his knee. "His father was always a man of a high stomach, ma'am," he said. Then facing towards Philip, "Your idea would be to return to the island."

"Yes," said Philip.

"Practice as an advocate, and push your way to insular preferment?"

"My father seemed to wish it, sir," said Philip.

The Ballawhaine turned back to Auntie Nan. "Well, Miss Christian?"

Auntie Nan fumbled the handle of her umbrella and began—"We were thinking, Peter—you see we know so little—now if his father had been living——"

The Ballawhaine coughed, scratched with his nail on his cheek, and said, "You wish me to put him with a barrister in chambers, is that it?"

With a nervous smile and a little laugh of relief Auntie Nan signified assent.

"You are aware that a step like that costs money. How much have you got to spend on it?"

"I'm afraid, Peter——"

"You thought I might find the expenses, eh?"

"It's so good of you to see it in the right way, Peter."

The Ballawhaine made a wry face. "Listen," he said dryly. "Ross has just gone to study for the English bar."

"Yes," said Auntie Nan eagerly, "and it was partly that——"

"Indeed!" said the Ballawhaine, raising his eyebrows. "I calculate that his course in London will cost me, one thing with another, more than a thousand pounds."

Auntie Nan lifted her gloved hands in amazement.

"That sum I am prepared to spend in order that my son, as an English barrister, may have a better chance——"

"Do you know, we were thinking of that ourselves, Peter?" said Auntie Nan.

"A better chance," the Ballawhaine continued, "of the few places open in the island than if he were brought up at the Manx bar only, which would cost me less than half as much."

"Oh! but the money will come back to you, both for Ross and Philip," said Auntie Nan.

The Ballawhaine coughed impatiently. "You don't read me," he said irritably. "These places are few, and Manx advocates are as thick as flies in a glue-pot. For every office there must be fifty applicants, but training counts for something, and influence for something, and family for something."

Auntie Nan began to be penetrated as by a chill.

"These," said the Ballawhaine, "I bring to bear for Ross, that he may distance all competitors. Do you read me now?"

"Read you, Peter?" said Auntie Nan.

The Ballawhaine fixed his hollow eye upon her, and said, "What do you ask me to do? You come here and ask me to provide, prepare, and equip a rival to my own son."

Auntie Nan had grasped his meaning at last.

"But gracious me, Peter," she said, "Philip is your own nephew, your own brother's son."

The Ballawhaine rubbed the side of his nose with his lean forefinger, and said, "Near is my shirt, but nearer is my skin."

Auntie Nan fixed her timid eyes upon him, and they grew brave in their gathering indignation. "His father is dead, and he is poor and friendless," she said.

"We've had differences on that subject before, mistress," he answered.

"And yet you begrudge him the little that would start him in life."

"My own has earlier claim, ma'am."

"Saving your presence, sir, let me tell you that every penny of the money you are spending on Ross would have been Philip's this day if things had gone different."

The Ballawhaine bit his lip. "Must I, for my sins, be compelled to put an end to this interview?"

He rose to go to the door. Philip rose also.

"Do you mean it?" said Auntie Nan. "Would you dare to turn me out of the house?"

"Come, Auntie, what's the use?" said Philip.

The Ballawhaine was drumming on the edge of the open door. "You are right, young man," he said, "a woman's hysteria is of *no* use."

"That will do, sir," said Philip in a firm voice.

The Ballawhaine put his hand familiarly on Philip's shoulder. "Try Bishop Wilson's theological college, my friend; its cheap and— —"

"Take your hand from him, Peter Christian," cried Auntie Nan. Her eyes flashed, her cheeks were aflame, her little gloved hands were clenched. "You made war between his father and your father, and when I would have made peace you prevented me. Your father is dead, and your brother is dead, and both died in hate that might have died in love, only for the lies you told and the deceit you practised. But they have gone where the mask falls from all faces, and they have met before this, eye to eye, and hand to hand. Yes, and they are looking down on you now, Peter Christian, and they know you at last for what you are and always have been—a deceiver and a thief."

By an involuntary impulse the Ballawhaine turned his eyes upward to the ceiling while she spoke, as if he had expected to see the ghosts of his father and his brother threatening him.

"Is the woman mad at all?" he cried; and the timid old lady, lifted out of herself by the flame of her anger, blazed at him again with a tongue of fire.

"You have done wrong, Peter Christian, much wrong; you've done wrong all your days, and whatever your motive, God will find it out, and on that secret place he will bring your punishment. If it was only greed, you've got your wages; but no good will they bring to you, for another will spend them, and you will see them wasted like water from the ragged rock. And if it was hate as well, you will live till it comes back on your own head like burning coal. I know it, I feel it," she cried, sweeping into the hall, "and sorry I am to say it before your own son, who ought to honour and respect his father, but can't; no, he can't and never will, or else he has a heart to match your own in wickedness, and no bowels of compassion at him either."

"Come, Auntie, come," said Philip, putting his arm about the old lady's waist. But she swerved round again to where the Ballawhaine came slinking behind him.

"Turn me out of the house, will you?" she cried. "The place where I lived fifteen years, and as mistress, too, until your evil deeds made you master. Many a good cry I've had that it's only a woman I am, and can do nothing on my own head. But I would rather be a woman that hasn't a roof to cover her than a man that can't warm to his own flesh and blood. Don't think I begrudge you your house, Peter Christian, though it was my old home, and I love it, for all I'm shown no respect in it I would have you to know, sir, that it isn't our houses we live in after all, but our hearts—our hearts, Peter Christian—do you hear me?—our hearts, and yours is full of darkness and dirt—and always will be, always will be."

"Come, come, Auntie, come," cried Philip again, and the sweet old thing, too gentle to hurt a fly, turned on him also with the fury of a wild-cat.

"Go along yourself with your 'come' and 'come' and 'come.' Say less and do more."

With that final outburst she swept down the steps and along the path, leaving Philip three paces behind, and the Ballawhaine with a terrified look under the stuffed cormorant in the fanlight above the open door.

The fiery mood lasted her half way home, and then broke down in a torrent of tears.

"Oh dear! oh dear!" she cried. "I've been too hasty. After all, he is your only relative. What shall I do now? Oh, what shall I do now?"

Philip was walking steadily half a step behind, and he had never once spoken since they left Ballawhaine.

"Pack my bag to-night, Auntie," said he with the voice of a man; "I shall start for Douglas by the coach to-morrow morning."

He sought out the best known of the Manx advocates, a college friend of his father's, and said to him, "I've sixty pounds a year, sir, from my mother's father, and my aunt has enough of her own to live on. Can I afford to pay your premium?"

The lawyer looked at him attentively for a moment, and answered, "No, you can't," and Philip's face began to fall.

"But I'll take you the five years for nothing, Mr. Christian," the wise man added, "and if you suit me, I'll give you wages after two."

II

Philip did not forget the task wherewith Pete had charged him. It is a familiar duty in the Isle of Man, and he who discharges it is known by a familiar name. They call him the *Dooiney Molla*—literally, the "man-praiser;" and his primary function is that of an informal, unmercenary, purely friendly and philanthropic matchmaker, introduced by the young man to persuade the parents of the young woman that he is a splendid fellow, with substantial possessions or magnificent prospects, and entirely fit to marry her. But he has a secondary function, less frequent, though scarcely less familiar; and it is that of lover by proxy, or intended husband by deputy, with duties of moral guardianship over the girl while the man himself is off "at the herrings," or away "at the mackerel," or abroad on wider voyages.

This second task, having gone through the first with dubious success, Philip discharged with conscientious zeal. The effects were peculiar. Their earliest manifestations were, as was most proper, on Philip and Kate themselves. Philip grew to be grave and wondrous solemn, for assuming the tone of guardian lifted his manners above all levity. Kate became suddenly very quiet and meek, very watchful and modest, soft of voice and most apt to blush. The girl who had hectored it over Pete and played little mistress over everybody else, grew to be like a dove under the eye of Philip. A kind of awe fell on her whenever he was near. She found it sweet to listen to his words of wisdom when he discoursed, and sweeter still to obey his will when he gave commands. The little wistful head was always turning in his direction; his voice was like joy-bells in her ears; his parting how under his lifted hat remained with her as a dream until the following day. She hardly knew what great change had been wrought in her, and her people at home were puzzled.

"Is it not very well you are, Kirry, woman?" said Grannie.

"Well enough, mother; why not?" said Kate.

"Is it the toothache that's plaguing you?"

"No."

"Then maybe it's the new hat in the window at Miss Clu-cas's?"

"Hould your tongue, woman," whispered Cæsar behind the back of his hand. "It's the Spirit that's working on the girl. Give it lave, mother; give it lave."

"Give it fiddlesticks," said Nancy Joe. "Give it brimstone and treacle and a cupful of wormwood and camomile."

When Philip and Kate were together, their talk was all of Pete. It was "Pete likes this," and "Pete hates that," and "Pete always says so and so." That was their way of keeping up the recollection of Pete's existence; and the uses they put poor Pete to were many and peculiar.

One night "The Manx Fairy" was merry and noisy with a "Scaltha," a Christmas supper given by the captain of a fishing-boat to the crew that he meant to engage for the season. Wives, sweethearts, and friends were there, and the customs and superstitions of the hour were honoured.

"Isn't it the funniest thing in the world, Philip?" giggled Kate from the back of the door, and a moment afterwards she was standing alone with him in the lobby, looking demurely down at his boots.

"I suppose I ought to apologise."

"Why so?"

"For calling you that."

"Pete calls me Philip. Why shouldn't you?"

The furtive eyes rose to the buttons of his waistcoat. "Well, no; there can't be much harm in calling you what Pete calls you, can there? But then—"

"Well?"

"He calls me Kate."

"Do you think he would like me to do so?"

"I'm sure he would."

"Shall we, then?"

"I wonder!"

"Just for Pete's sake?"

"Just."

"Kate!"

"Philip!"

They didn't know what they felt. It was something exquisite, something delicious; so sweet, so tender, they could only laugh as if some one had tickled them.

"Of course, we need not do it except when we are quite by ourselves," said Kate.

"Oh no, of course not, only when we are quite alone," said Philip.

Thus they threw dust into each other's eyes, and walked hand in hand on the edge of a precipice.

The last day of the old year after Pete's departure found Philip attending to his duty.

"Are you going to put the new year in anywhere, Philip?" said Kate, from the door of the porch.

"I should be the first-foot here, only I'm no use as a qualtagh," said Philip.

"Why not?"

"I'm a fair man, and would bring you no luck, you know."

"Ah!"

There was silence for a moment, and then Kate cried "*I* know."

"Yes?"

"Come for Pete—he's dark enough, anyway."

Philip was much impressed. "That's a good idea," he said gravely. "Being qualtagh for Pete is a good idea. His first New Year from home, too, poor fellow!"

"Exactly," said Kate.

"Shall I, then?"

"I'll expect you at the very stroke of twelve."

Philip was going off. "And, Philip!"

"Yes?"

Then a low voice, so soft, so sweet, so merry, came from the doorway into the dark, "I'll be standing at the door of the dairy."

Philip began to feel alarm, and resolved to take for the future a lighter view of his duties. He would visit "The Manx Fairy" less frequently. As soon as the Christmas holidays were over he would devote himself to his studies, and come back to Sulby no more for half a year. But the Manx Christmas is long. It begins on the 24th of December, and only ends for good on the 6th of January. In the country places, which still preserve the old traditions, the culminating day is Twelfth Day. It is then that they "cut off the fiddler's head," and play valentines, which they call the "Goggans." The girls set a row of mugs on the hearth in front of the fire, put something into each of them as a symbol of a trade, and troop out to the stairs. Then the boys change the order of the mugs, and the girls come back blindfold, one by one, to select their goggans. According to the goggans they lay hands on, so will be the trades of their husbands.

At this game, played at "The Manx Fairy" on the last night of Philip's holiday, Csesar being abroad on an evangelising errand, Kate was expected to draw water, but she drew a quill.

"A pen! A pen!" cried the boys. "Who says the girl is to marry a sailor? The ship isn't built that's to drown her husband."

"Good-night all," said Philip.

"Good-night, Mr. Christian, good-night, sir," said the boys.

Kate slipped after him to the door. "Going so early, Philip?"

"I've to be back at Douglas to-morrow morning," said Philip.

"I suppose we shan't see you very soon?"

"No, I must set to work in earnest now."

"A fortnight—a month may be?"

"Yes, and six months—I intend to do nothing else for half a year."

"That's a long time, isn't it, Philip?"

"Not so long as I've wasted."

"Wasted? So you call it wasted? Of course, it's nothing to me—but there's your aunt——"

"A man can't always be dangling about women," said Philip.

Kate began to laugh.

"What are you laughing at?"

"I'm so glad I'm a girl," said Kate.

"Well, so am I," said Philip.

"Are you?"

It came at his face like a flash of lightning, and Philip stammered, "I mean—that is—you know—what about Pete?"

"Oh, is that all? Well, good-night, if you must go. Shall I bring you the lantern? No need? Starlight, is it? You can see your way to the gate quite plainly? Very well, if you don't want showing. Good-night!"

The last words, in an injured tone, were half lost behind the closing door.

But the heart of a girl is a dark forest, and Kate had determined that, work or no work, so long a spell as six months Philip should not be away.

III

One morning in the late spring there came to Douglas a startling and most appalling piece of news—-Ross Christian was constantly seen at "The Manx Fairy." On the evening of that day Philip reappeared at Sulby. He had come down in high wrath, inventing righteous speeches by the way on plighted troths and broken pledges. Ross was there in lacquered boots, light kid gloves, frock coat, and pepper and salt trousers, leaning with elbow on the counter, that he might talk to Kate, who was serving. Philip had never before seen her at that task, and his indignation was extreme. He was more than ever sure that Grannie was a simpleton and Cæsar a brazen hypocrite.

Kate nodded gaily to him as he entered, and then continued her conversation with Ross. There was a look in her eyes that was new to him, and it caused him to change his purpose. He would not be indignant, he would be cynical, he would be nasty, he would wait his opportunity and put in with some cutting remark. So, at Cæsar's invitation and Grannie's welcome, he pushed through the bar-room to the kitchen, exchanged salutations, and then sat down to watch and to listen.

The conversation beyond the glass partition was eager and enthusiastic. Ross was fluent and Kate was vivacious.

"My friend Monty?"

"Yes; who is Monty?"

"He's the centre of the Fancy."

"The Fancy!"

"Ornaments of the Ring, you know. Come now, surely you know the Ring, my dear. His rooms in St. James's Street are full of them every night. All sorts, you know—featherweights, and heavy-weights, and greyhounds. And the faces! My goodness, you should see them. Such worn-out old images. Knowledge boxes all awry, mouths crooked, and noses that have had the upper-cut. But good men all; good to take their gruel, you know. Monty will have nothing else about him. He was Tom Spring's packer. Never heard of Tom Spring? Tom of Bedford, the incorruptible, you know, only he fought cross that day. Monty lost a thousand, and Tom keeps a public in Holborn now with pictures of the Fancy round the walls."

Then Kate, with a laugh, said something which Philip did not catch, because Cæsar was rustling the newspaper he was reading.

"Ladies come?" said Ross. "Girls at Monty's suppers? Rather! what should you think? Cleopatra—but you ought to be there. I must be getting off myself very soon. There's a supper coming off next week at Handsome Honey's. Who's Honey? Proprietor of a night-house in the Haymarket. Night-house? You come and see, my dear."

Cæsar dropped the newspaper and looked across at Philip. The gaze was long and embarrassing, and, for want of better conversation, Philip asked Cæsar if he was thinking.

"Aw, thinking, thinking, and thinking again, sir," said Cæsar. Then, drawing his chair nearer to Philip's, he added, in a half whisper, "I'm getting a bit of a skute into something, though. See yonder? They're calling his father a miser. The man's racking his tenants and starving his land. But I believe enough the young brass lagh (a weed) is choking the ould grain."

Cæsar, as he spoke, tipped his thumb over his shoulder in the direction of Ross, and, seeing this, Ross interrupted his conversation with Kate to address himself to her father.

"So you've been reading the paper, Mr. Cregeen?"

"Aw, reading and reading," said Cæsar grumpily. Then in another tone, "You're home again from London, sir? Great doings yonder, they're telling me. Battles, sir, great battles."

Ross elevated his eyebrows. "Have you heard of them then?" he asked.

"Aw, heard enough," said Cæsar, "meetings, and conferences, and conventions, and I don't know what."

"Oh, oh, I see," said Ross, with a look at Kate.

"They're doing without hell in England now-a-days—that's a quare thing, sir. Conditional immorality they're calling it—the singlerest thing I know. Taking hell away drops the tailboard out of a man's religion, eh?"

The time for closing came, and Philip had waited in vain. Only one cut had come his way, and that had not been his own. As he rose to go, Kate had said, "We didn't expect to see you again for six months, Mr. Christian."

"So it seems," said Philip, and Kate laughed a little, and that was all the work of his evening, and the whole result of his errand.

Cæsar was waiting for him in the porch. His face was white, and it twitched visibly. It was plain to see that the natural man was fighting in Cæsar. "Mr. Christian, sir," said he, "are you the gentleman that came here to speak to me for Peter Quilliam?"

"I am," said Philip.

"Then do you remember the ould Manx saying, 'Perhaps the last dog may be catching the hare?'"

"Leave it to me, Mr. Cregeen," said Philip through his teeth.

Half a minute afterwards he was swinging down the dark road homewards, by the side of Ross, who was drawling along with his cold voice.

"So you've started on your light-weight handicap, Philip. Father was monstrous unreasonable that day. Seemed to think I was coming back here to put my shoulder out for your high bailiffships and bum-bailiffships and heaven knows what. You're welcome to the lot for me, Philip. That girl's wonderful, though. It's positively miraculous, too; she's the living picture of a girl of my friend Montague's. Eyes, hair, that nervous movement of the mouth—everything. Old man looked glum enough, though. Poor little woman. I suppose she's past praying for. The old hypocrite will hold her like a dove in the claws of a buzzard hawk till she throws herself away on some Manx omathaun. It's the way with half these pretty creatures—they're wasted."

Philip's blood was boiling. "Do you call it being wasted when a good girl is married to an honest man?" he asked.

"I do; because a girl like this can never marry the right man. The man who is worthy of her cannot marry her, and the man who marries her isn't worthy of her. It's like this, Philip. She's young, she's pretty, perhaps beautiful, has manners and taste, and some refinement. The man of her own class is clumsy and ignorant, and stupid and poor. She doesn't want him, and the man she does want the man she's fit for—daren't marry her; it would be social suicide."

"And so," said Philip bitterly, "to save the man above from social suicide, the girl beneath must choose moral death—is that it?"

Ross laughed. "Do you know I thought old Jeremiah was at you in the corner there, Philip. But look at it straight. Here's a girl like that. Two things are open to her—two only. Say she marries your Manx fellow, what follows? A thatched cottage three fields back from the mountain road, two rooms, a cowhouse, a crock, a dresser, a press, a form, a three-legged stool, an armchair, and a clock with a dirty face, hanging on a nail in the wall. Milking, weeding, digging, ninepence a day, and a can of buttermilk, with a lump of butter thrown in. Potatoes, herrings, and barley bonnag. Year one, a baby, a boy; year two, another baby, a girl; year three, twins; year four, barefooted children squalling, dirty house, man grumbling, woman distracted, measles, hooping-cough; a journey at the tail of a cart to the bottom of the valley, and the awful words 'I am the——'"

"Hush man!" said Philip. They were passing Lezayre churchyard. When they had left it behind, he added, with a grim curl of the lip, which was lost in the darkness, "Well, that's one side. What's the other?"

"Life," said Ross. "Short and sweet, perhaps. Everything she wants, everything she can wish for—five years, four years, three years—what matter?"

"And then?"

"Every one for himself and God for us all, my boy. She's as happy as the day while it lasts, lifts her head like a rosebud in the sun——"

"Then drops it, I suppose, like a rose-leaf in the mud." Ross laughed again. "Yes, it's a fact, old Jeremiah *has* been at you, Philip. Poor little Kitty——"

"Keep the girl's name out of it, if you please."

Ross gave a long whistle. "I was only saying the poor little woman——"

"It's damnable, and I'll have no more of it."

"There's no duty on speech, I hope, in your precious Isle of Man."

"There is, though," said Philip, "a duty of decency and honour, and to name that girl, foolish as she is, in the same breath with your women—But here, listen to me. Best tell you now, so there may be no mistake and no excuse. Miss Cregeen is to be married to a friend of mine. I needn't say who he is—he comes close enough to you at all events. When he's at home, he's able to take care of his own affairs; but while he's abroad I've got to see that no harm comes to his promised wife. I mean to do it, too. Do you understand me, Ross? I mean to do it. Good night!"

They were at the gate of Ballawhaine by this time, and Ross went through it giggling.

IV

The following evening found Philip at "The Manx Fairy" again. Ross was there as usual, and he was laughing and talking in a low tone with Kate. This made Philip squirm on his chair, but Kate's behaviour tortured him. Her enjoyment of the man's jests was almost uproarious. She was signalling to him and peering up at him gaily. Her conduct disgusted Philip. It seemed to him an aggravation of her offence that as often as he caught the look of her face there was a roguish twinkle in the eye on his side, and a deliberate cast in his direction. This open disregard of the sanctity of a pledged word, this barefaced indifference to the presence of him who stood to represent it, was positively indecent. This was what women were! Deceit was bred in their bones.

It added to Philip's gathering wrath that Cæsar, who sat in shirt-sleeves making up his milling accounts from slates ciphered with crosses, and triangles, and circles, and half circles, was lifting his eyes from time to time to look first at them and then at him, with an expression of contempt.

At a burst of fresh laughter and a shot of the bright eyes, Philip surged up to his feet, thrust himself between Ross and Kate, turned his back on him and his face to her, and said in a peremptory voice, "Come into the parlour instantly—I have something to say to you."

"Oh, indeed!" said Kate.

But she came, looking mischievous and yet demure, with her head down but her eyes peering under their long upper lashes.

"Why don't you send this fellow about his business?" said Philip.

Kate looked up in blank surprise. "What fellow?" she said.

"What fellow?" said Philip, "why, this one that is shillyshallying with you night after night."

"You can never mean your own cousin, Philip?" said Kate.

"More's the pity if he is my cousin, but he's no fit company for you."

"I'm sure the gentleman is polite enough."

"So's the devil himself."

"He can behave and keep his temper, anyway."

"Then it's the only thing he can keep. He can't keep his character or his credit or his honor, and you should not encourage him."

Kate's under lip began to show the inner half. "Who says I encourage him?"

"I do."

"What right have you?"

"Haven't I seen you with my own eyes?"

Kate grew defiant. "Well, and what if you have?"

"Then you are a jade and a coquette."

The word hissed out like steam from a kettle. Kate saw it coming and took it full in the face. She felt an impulse to scream with laughter, so she seized her opportunity and cried.

Philip's temper began to ebb. "That man would be a poor bargain, Kate, if he were twenty times the heir of Ballawhaine. Can't you gather from his conversation what his life and companions are? Of course it's nothing to me, Kate— —"

"No, it's nothing to you," whimpered Kate, from behind both hands.

"I've no right— —"

"Of course not; you've no right," said Kate, and she stole a look sideways.

"Only— —"

Philip did not see the glance that came from the corner of Kate's eye.

"When a girl forgets a manly fellow, who happens to be abroad, for the first rascal that comes along with his dirty lands—"

Down went the hands with an impatient fling. "What are his lands to me?"

"Then it's my duty as a friend— —"

"Duty indeed! Just what every old busybody says."

Philip gripped her wrist. "Listen to me. If you don't send this man packing— —"

"You are hurting me. Let go my arm."

Philip flung it aside and said, "What do I care?"

"Then why do you call me a coquette?"

"Do as you like."

"So I will. Philip! Philip! Phil! He's gone."

It was twenty miles by coach and rail from Douglas to Sulby, but Philip was back at "The Manx Fairy" the next evening also. He found a saddle-horse linked to the gate-post and Ross inside the house with a riding-whip in his hand, beating the leg of his riding-breeches.

When Philip appeared, Kate began to look alarmed, and Ross to look ugly. Cæsar, who was taking his tea in the ingle, was having an unpleasant passage with Grannie in side-breaths by the fire.

"Bad, bad, a notorious bad liver and dirty with the tongue," said Cæsar.

"Chut, father!" said Grannie. "The young man's civil enough, and girls will be girls. What's a word or a look or a laugh when you're young and have a face that's fit for anything."

"Better her face should be pitted with smallpox than bring her to the pit of hell," said Cæsar. "All flesh is grass: the grass withereth, the flower fadeth."

Nancy Joe came from the dairy at that moment. "Gracious me I did you see that now?" she said. "I wonder at Kitty. But it's the way of the men, smiling and smiling and maning nothing."

"Hm! They mane a dale," growled Cæsar.

Ross had recovered from his uneasiness at Philip's entrance, and was engaged in some narration whereof the only words that reached the kitchen were *I know* and *I know* repeated frequently.

"You seem to know a dale, sir," shouted Cæsar; "do you know what it is to be saved?"

There was silence for a moment, and then Ross, polishing his massive signet ring on his corduroy waistcoat, said, "Is that the old gentleman's complaint, I wonder?"

"My husband is a local preacher and always strong for salvation," said Grannie by way of peace.

"Is that all?" said Ross. "I thought perhaps he had taken more wine than the sacrament."

"You're my cross, woman," muttered Cæsar, "but no cross no crown."

"Lave women's matters alone, father; it'll become you better," said Grannie.

"Laugh as you like, Mistress Cregeen; there's One above, there's One above."

Ross had resumed his conversation with Kate, who was looking frightened. And listening with all his ears, Philip caught the substance of what was said.

"I'm due back by this time. There's the supper at Handsome Honey's, not to speak of the everlasting examinations. But somehow I can't tear myself away. Why not? Can't you guess? No? Not a notion? I would go to-morrow—Kitty, a word in your ear——"

"I believe in my heart that man is for kissing her," said Cæsar. "If he does, then by—he's done it! Hould, sir."

Cæsar had risen to his feet, and in a moment the house was in an uproar. Ross lifted his head like a cock. "Were you speaking to me, mister?" he asked.

"I was, and don't demane yourself like that again," said Cæsar.

"Like what?" said Ross.

"Paying coort to a girl that isn't fit for you."

Ross lifted his hat, "Do you mean this young lady?"

"No young lady at all, sir, but the daughter of a plain, respectable man that isn't going to see her fooled. Your hat to your head, sir. You'll be wanting it for the road."

"Father!" cried Kate, in a voice of fear.

Cæsar turned his rough shoulder and said, "Go to your room, ma'am, and keep it for a week."

"You may go," said Ross. "I'll spare the old simpleton for your sake, Kate."

"You'll spare me, sir?" cried Cæsar. "I've seen the day—but thank the Lord for restraining grace! Spare me? If you had said as much five-and-twenty years ago, sir, your head would have gone ringing against the wall."

"I'll spare you no more, then," said Ross. "Take that—and that."

Amid screams from the women, two sounding blows fell on Cæsar's face. At the next instant Philip was standing between the two men.

"Come this way," he said, addressing Ross.

"If I like," Ross answered.

"This way, I tell you," said Philip.

Ross snapped his fingers. "As you please," he said, and then followed Philip out of the house.

Kate had run upstairs in terror, but five minutes afterwards she was on the road, with a face full of distress, and a shawl over head and shoulders. At the bridge she met Kelly, the postman.

"Which way have they gone," she panted, "the young Ballawhaine and Philip Christian?"

"I saw them heading down to the Curragh," said Kelly, and Kate in the shawl, flew like a bird over the ground in that direction.

V

The two young men went on without a word. Philip walked with long strides three paces in front, with head thrown back, pallid face and contracted features, mouth firmly shut, arms stiff by his side, and difficult and audible breathing. Ross slouched behind with an air of elaborate carelessness, his horse beside him, the reins over its head and round his arm, the riding-whip under his other arm-pit, and both his hands deep in the breeches pockets. There was no road the way they went, but only a cart track, interrupted here and there by a gate, and bordered by square turf pits half full of water.

The days were long and the light was not yet failing. Beyond the gorse, the willows, the reeds, the rushes and the sally bushes of the flat land, the sun was setting over a streak of gold on the sea. They had left behind them the smell of burning turf, of crackling sticks, of fish, and of the cowhouse, and were come into the atmosphere of flowering gorse and damp scraa soil and brine.

"Far enough, aren't we?" shouted Ross, but Philip pushed on. He drew up at last in an open space, where the gorse had been burnt away and its black remains desolated the surface and killed the odours of life. There was not a house near, not a landmark in sight, except a windmill on the sea's verge, and the ugly tower of a church, like the funnel of a steamship between sea and sky.

"We're alone at last," he said hoarsely.

"We are," said Ross, interrupting the whistling of a tune, "and now that you've got me here, perhaps you'll be good enough to tell me what we've come for."

Philip made no more answer than to strip himself of his coat and waistcoat.

"You're never going to make a serious business of this stupid affair?" said Ross, leaning against the horse and slapping the sole of one foot with the whip.

"Take off your coat," said Philip in a thick voice.

"Can I help it if a pretty girl— —" began Ross.

"Will you strip?" cried Philip.

Ross laughed. "Ah! now I remember our talk of the other night. But you don't mean to say," he said, flipping at the flies at the horse's head, "that because the little woman is forgetting the curmudgeon that's abroad— —"

Philip strode up to him with clenched hands and quivering lips and said, "Will you fight?"

Ross laughed again, but the blood was in his face, and he said tauntingly, "I wouldn't distress myself, man. Daresay I'll be done with the girl before the fellow— —"

"You're a scoundrel," cried Philip, "and if you won't stand up to me— —"

Ross flung away his whip. "If I must, I must," he said, and then threw the horse's reins round the charred arm of a half-destroyed gorse tree.

A minute afterwards the young men stood face to face.

"Stop," said Ross, "let me tell you first; it's only fair. Since I went up to London I've learnt a thing or two. I've stood up before men that can strip a picture; I've been opposite talent and I can peck a bit, but I've never heard that you can stop a blow."

"Are you ready?" cried Philip.

"As you will. You shall have one round, you'll want no more."

The young men looked badly matched. Ross, in riding-breeches and shirt, with red bullet head and sprawling feet, arms like an oak and veins like willow boughs. Philip in shirt and knickerbockers, with long fair hair, quivering face, and delicate figure. It was strength and some skill against nerve alone.

Like a rush of wind Philip came on, striking right and left, and was driven back by a left-hand body-blow.

"There, you've got it," said Ross, smiling benignly. "Didn't I tell you? That's old Bristol Bull to begin with."

Philip rushed on again, and came back with a smashing blow that cut his nether lip.

"You've got a second," said Ross. "Have you had enough?"

Philip did not hear, but sprang fiercely at Ross once more. The next instant he was on the ground. Then Ross took on a manner of utter contempt. "I can't keep on flipping at you all night."

"Mock me when you've beaten me," said Philip, and he was on his feet again, somewhat blown, but fresh as to spirit and doggedly resolute.

"Toe the scratch, then," said Ross. "I must say you're good at your gruel."

Philip flung himself on his man a third time, and fell more heavily than before, under a flush hit that seemed to bury itself in his chest.

"I can't go on fighting a man that's as good for nothing as my old grandmother," said Ross.

But his contempt was abating; he was growing uneasy; Philip was before him as fierce as ever.

"Fight your equal," he cried.

"I'll fight you," growled Philip.

"You're not fit. Give it up. And look, the dark is falling."

"There's enough daylight yet. Come on."

"Nobody is here to shame you."

"Come on, I say."

Philip did not wait, but sprang on his man like a tiger. Ross met his blow, dodged, feinted; they gripped, swinging to and fro; there was a struggle, and Philip fell again with a dull thud against the ground.

"Will you stop now?" said Ross.

"No, no, no," cried Philip, leaping to his feet.

"I'll eat you up. I'm a glutton, I can tell you." But his voice trembled, and Philip, blind with passion, laughed.

"You'll be hurt," said Ross.

"What of that?" said Philip.

"You'll be killed."

"I'm willing."

Ross tried to laugh mockingly, but the hoarse gurgle choked in his throat. He began to tremble. "This man doesn't know when he's mauled," he muttered, and after a loud curse he stood up afresh, with a craven and shifty look. His blows fell like scorching missiles, but Philip took them like a rock scoured with shingle, raining blood like water, but standing firm.

"What's the use?" cried Ross; "drop it."

"I'll drop myself first," said Philip.

"If you won't give it up, I will," said Ross.

"You shan't," said Philip.

"Take your victory if you like."

"I won't."

"Say you've licked me."

"I'll do it first," said Philip.

Ross laughed long and riotously, but he was trembling like a whipped cur. With a blob of foam on his lips he came up, collecting all his strength, and struck Philip a blow on the forehead that fell with the sound of a hammer on a coffin.

"Are you done?" he snuffled.

"No, by God," cried Philip, black as ink with the burnt gorse from the ground, except where the blood ran red on him.

"This man means to kill me," mumbled Ross. He looked round shiftily, and said, "I mean no harm by the girl."

"You're a liar!" cried Philip.

With a glance of deep malignity, Ross closed with Philip again. It was now a struggle of right with wrong as well as nerve with strength. The sun had set under the sea, the sally bushes were shivering in the twilight, a flight of rooks were screaming overhead. Blows were no more heard. Ross gripped Philip in a venomous embrace, and dragged him on to one knee. Philip rose, Ross doubled round his waist, pushing him backward, and fell heavily on his breast, shouting with the growl of a beast, "You'll fight me, will you? Get up, get up!"

Philip did not rise, and Ross began dragging and lunging at him with brutal ferocity, when suddenly, where he bent double, a blow fell on his ear from behind, another and another, a hand gripped his shirt collar and choked him, and a voice cried, "Let go, you brute, let go, let go."

Ross dropped Philip and swung himself round to return the attack.

It was the girl. "Oh, it's you, is it?" he panted. She was like a fury. "You brute, you beast, you toad," she cried, and then threw herself over Philip.

He was unconscious. She lifted his head on to her lap, and, lost to all shame, to all caution, to all thought but one thought, she kissed him on the cheek, on the lips, on the eyes, on the forehead, crying, "Philip! oh, Philip, Philip!"

Ross was shuddering beside them. "Let me look at him," he faltered, but Kate fired back with a glance like an arrow, and said, screaming like a sea-gull, "If you touch him again I'll strangle you."

Ross caught a glimpse of Philip's face, and he was terrified. Going to a turf pit, he dipped both hands in the dub, and brought some water. "Take this," he said, "for Heaven's sake let me bathe his head."

He dashed the water on the pallid forehead, and then withdrew his eyes, while the girl coaxed Philip back to consciousness with fresh kisses and pleading words.

"Is he breathing? Feel his heart. Any pulsation? Oh, God!" said Ross, "it wasn't my fault." He looked round with wild eyes; he meditated flight.

"Is he better yet?"

"What's it to you, you coward?" said Kate, with a burning glance. She went on with her work: "Come then, dear, come, come now."

Philip opened his eyes in a vacant stare, and rose on his elbow. Then Kate fell back from him immediately, and began to cry quietly, being all woman now, and her moral courage gone again in an instant.

But the moral courage of Mr. Ross came back as quickly. He began to sneer and to laugh lightly, picked up his riding-whip and strode over to his horse.

"Are you hurt?" asked Kate, in a low tone.

"Is it Kate?" said Philip.

At the sound of his voice, in that low whisper, Kate's tears came streaming down.

"I hope youll forgive me," she said. "I should have taken your warning."

She wiped his face with the loose sleeve of her dress, and then he struggled to his feet.

"Lean on me, Philip."

"No, no, I can walk."

"Do take my arm."

"Oh no, Kate, I'm strong enough."

"Just to please me."

"Well—very well."

Ross looked on with jealous rage. His horse, frightened by the fight, had twirled round and round till the reins were twisted into a knot about the gorse stump, and as he liberated the beast he flogged it back till it flew around him. Then he vaulted to the saddle, tugged at the curb, and the horse reared. "Down," he cried with an oath, and lashed brutally at the horse's head.

Meantime Kate, going past him with Philip on her arm, was saying softly, "Are you feeling better, Philip?"

And Ross, looking on in sulky meditation, sent a harsh laugh out of his hot throat, and said, "Oh, you can make your mind easy about *him*, if your other man fights for you like that you'll do. Thought you'd have three of them, did you? Or perhaps you only wanted me for your decoy? Why don't you kiss him now, when he can know it? But he's a beauty to take care of you for somebody else. Fighting for the other one, eh? Stuff and humbug! Take him home, and the curse of Judas on the brace of you."

So saying, he burst into wild, derisive laughter, flogged his horse on the ears and the nose, shouted "Down, you brute, down!" and shot off at a gallop across the open Curragh.

Philip and Kate stood where he had left them till he had disappeared in the mist rising off the marshy land, and the hud of his horse's hoofs could be no more heard. Their heads were down, and though their arms were locked, their faces were turned half aside. There was silence for some time. The girl's eyelids quivered; her look was anxious and helpless. Then Philip said, "Let us go home," and they began to walk together.

Not another word did they speak. Neither looked into the other's eyes. Their entwined arms slackened a little in a passionless asundering, yet both felt that they must hold tight or they would fall. It was almost as if Ross's parting taunt had uncovered their hearts to each other, and revealed to themselves their secret. They were like other children of the garden of Eden, driven out and stripped naked.

At the bridge they met Cæsar, Grannie, Nancy Joe, and half the inhabitants of Sulby, abroad with lanterns in search of them.

"They're here," cried Cæsar. "You've chastised him, then! You'd bait his head off, I'll go bail. And I believe enough you'll be forgiven, sir. Yonder blow was almost bitterer than flesh can bear. Before my days of grace—but, praise the Lord for His restraining hand, the very minute my anger was up He crippled me in the hip with rheumatics. But what's this?" holding the lantern over his head; "there's blood on your face, sir?"

"A scratch—it's nothing," said Philip.

"It's the women that's in every mischief," said Cæsar.

"Lord bless me, aren't the women as good as the men?" said Nancy.

"H'm," said Cæsar. "We're told that man was made a little lower than the angels, but about women we're just left to our own conclusions."

"Scripture has nothing to do with Ross Christian, father," said Grannie.

"The Lord forbid it," said Cæsar. "What can you get from a cat but his skin? And doesn't the man come from Christian Ballawhaine!"

"If it comes to that, though, haven't we all come from Adam?" said Grannie.

"Yes; and from Eve too, more's the pity," said Cæsar.

VI

For some time thereafter Philip went no more to Sulby. He had a sufficient excuse. His profession made demand of all his energies. When he was not at work in Douglas he was expected to be at home with his aunt at Ballure. But neither absence nor the lapse of years served to lift him out of the reach of temptation. He had one besetting provocation to remembrance—one duty which forbade him to forget Kate—his pledge to Pete, his office as *Dooiney Molla*. Had he not vowed to keep guard over the girl? He must do it. The trust was a sacred one.

Philip found a way out of his difficulty. The post was an impersonal and incorruptible go-between, so he wrote frequently. Sometimes he had news to send, for, to avoid the espionage of Cæsar, intelligence of Pete came through him; occasionally he had love-letters to enclose; now and then he had presents to pass on. When such necessity did not arise, he found it agreeable to keep up the current of correspondence. At Christmas he sent Christmas cards, on Midsummer Day a bunch of moss roses, and even on St. Valentine's Day a valentine. All this was in discharge of his duty, and everything he did was done in the name of Pete. He persuaded himself that he sank his own self absolutely. Having denied his eyes the very sight of the girl's face, he stood erect in the belief that he was a true and loyal friend.

Kate was less afraid and less ashamed. She took the presents from Pete and wore them for Philip. In her secret heart she thought no shame of this. The years gave her a larger flow of life, and made out of the bewitching girl a splendid woman, brought up to the full estate of maidenly beauty.

This change wrought by time on her bodily form caused the past to seem to her a very long way off. Something had occurred that made her a different being. She was like the elder sister of that laughing girl who had known Pete. To think of that little sister as having a kind of control over her was impossible. Kate never did think of it.

Nevertheless, she held her tongue. Her people were taken in by the episode of Ross Christian. According to their view, Kate loved the man and still longed for him, and that was why she never talked of Pete. Philip was disgusted with her unfaithfulness to his friend, and that was the reason of his absence. She never talked of Philip either, but they, on their part, talked of him perpetually, and fed her secret passion with his praises. Thus for three years these two were like two prisoners in neighbouring cells, very close and yet very far apart, able to hear each other's voices, yet never to see each other's faces, yearning to come together and to touch, but unable to do so because of the wall that stood between.

Since the fight, Cæsar had removed her from all duties of the inn, and one day in the spring she was in the gable house peeling rushes to make tallow candles when Kelly, the postman, passed by the porch, where Nancy Joe was cleaning the candle-irons.

"Heard the newses, Nancy?" said Kelly. "Mr. Philip Christian is let off two years' time and called to the bar."

Nancy looked grave. "I'm sure the young gentleman is that quiet and studdy," she said. "What are they doing on him?"

"Only making him a full advocate, woman," said Kelly.

"You don't say?" said Nancy.

"He passed his examination before the Govenar's man yesterday."

"Aw, there now!"

"I took the letter to Ballure this evening."

"It's like you would, Mr. Kelly. That's the boy for you. I'm always saying it. 'Deed I am, though, but there's ones here that won't have it at all, at all."

"Miss Kate, you mane? We know the raison. He's lumps in her porridge, woman. Good-day to you, Nancy."

"Yes, it's doing a nice day enough, Mr. Kelly," said Nancy, and the postman passed on.

Kate came gliding out with a brush in her hand. "What was the postman saying?"

"That—Mr.—Philip—Christian—has been passing—for an advocate," said Nancy deliberately.

Kate's eyes glistened, and her lips quivered with delight; but she only said, with an air of indifference, "Was that all his news, then?"

"All? D'ye say all?" said Nancy, digging away at the candle-irons. "Listen to the girl! And him that good to her while her promist man's away!"

Kate shelled her rush, and said, with a sigh and a sly look, "I'm afraid you think a deal too much of him, Nancy."

"Then I'll be making mends," said Nancy, "for some that's thinking a dale too little."

"I'm quite at a loss to know what you see in him," said Kate.

"Now, you don't say!" said Nancy with scorching irony. Then, banging her irons, she added, "I'm not much of a woman for a man myself. They're only poor helpless creatures anyway, and I don't approve of them. But if I was for putting up with one of the sort, he wouldn't have legs and arms like a dolly, and a face like curds and whey, and coat and trousers that loud you can hear them coming up the street."

With this parting shot at Ross Christian, Nancy flung into the house, thinking she had given Kate a dressing that she would never forget. Kate was radiant. Such abuse was honey on her lips, such scoldings were joy-bells in her ears. She took silent delight in provoking these attacks. They served her turn both ways, bringing her delicious joy at the praise of Philip, and at the same time preserving her secret.

VII

Latter that day Cæsar came in from the mill with the startling intelligence that Philip was riding up on the highroad.

"Goodness mercy!" cried Nancy, and she fled away to wash her face. Grannie with a turn of the hand settled her cap, and smoothed her grey hair under it. Kate herself had disappeared like a flash of light; but as Philip dismounted at the gate, looking taller, and older, and paler, and more serious, but raising his cap from his fair head and smiling a smile like sunshine, she was coming leisurely out of the porch with a bewitching hat over her wavy black hair and a hand-basket over her arm.

Then there was a little start of surprise and recognition, a short catch of quick breath and nervous salutations.

"I'm going round to the nests," she said. "I suppose you'll step in to see mother."

"Time enough for that," said Philip. "May I help you with the eggs first? Besides, I've something to tell you."

"Is it that you're 'admitted?'" said Kate.

"That's nothing," said Philip. "Only the A B C, you know. Getting ready to begin, so to speak."

They walked round to the stackyard, and he tied up his horse and gave it hay. Then, while they poked about for eggs on hands and knees among the straw, under the stacks and between the bushes, she said she hoped he would have success, and he answered that success was more than a hope to him now—it was a sort of superstition. She did not understand this, but looked up at him from all fours with brightening eyes, and said, "What a glorious thing it is to be a man!"

"Is it?" said Philip. "And yet I remember somebody who said she wasn't sorry to be a girl."

"Did I?" said Kate. "But that was long ago. And *I* remember somebody else who pretended he was glad I was."

"That was long ago too," said Philip, and both laughed nervously.

"What strange things girls are—and boys!" said Kate with a matronly sigh, burying her face in a nest where a hen was clucking and two downy chicks were peeping from her wing.

They went through to the orchard, where the trees were breaking into eager blossoms.

"I've another letter for you from Pete," said Philip.

"So?" said Kate.

"Here it is," said Philip.

"Won't you read it?" said Kate.

"But it's yours; surely a girl doesn't want anybody else——"

"Ah! but you're different, though; you know everything—and besides—read it aloud, Philip."

With her basket of eggs on one arm, and the other hand on the outstretched arm of an apple-tree, she waited while he read:

"Dearest Kitty,—How's yourself, darling, and how's Philip, and how's Grannie? I'm getting on tremendous. They're calling me Captain now—Capt'n Pete. Sort of overseer at the Diamond Mines outside Kimberley. Regular gentleman's life and no mistake. Nothing to do but sit under a monstrous big umbrella, with a paper in your fist, like a chairman, while twenty Kaffirs do the work. Just a bit of a tussle now and then to keep you from dropping off. When a Kaffir turns up a diamond, you grab it, and mark it on the time-sheet against his name. They've got their own outlandish ones, but we always christen them ourselves—Sixpence, Seven Waistcoats, Shoulder-of-Mutton, Twopenny Trotter—anything you like. When a Kaffir strikes a diamond, he gets a commission, and so does his overseer. I'm afraid I'm going to be getting terrible rich soon. Tell the old man I'll be buying that har-monia yet. They are a knowing lot, though, and if they can get up a dust to smuggle a stone when you're not looking, they will. Then they sell it to the blackleg Boers, and you've got to raise your voice like an advocate to get it back somehow. But the Boers can't do no harm to you with their fists at all—it's playing. They're a dirty lot, wonderful straight like some of the lazy Manx ones, especially Black Tom. When they see us down at the river washing, they say, 'What dirty people the English must be if they have to wash themselves three times a day—we only do it once a week.' When a Kaffir steals a stone we usually court-martial him, but I don't hold with it, as the floggers on the compound can't be trusted; so I always lick my own niggers, being more kinder, and if anybody does anything against me, they lynch him."

Kate made a little patient sigh and turned away her head, while Philip, in a halting voice, went on—

"Darling Kitty, I am longing mortal for a sight of your sweet face. When the night comes, and I'll be lying in the huts—boards on the ground, and good canvas, and everything comfortable—says I to the boys, 'Shut your faces, men, and let a poor chap sleep;' but they never twig the darkness of my meaning. I'll only be wanting a bit of quiet for thinking of.... with the stars atwinkling down.... She's looking at that one.... Shine on my angel...."

"Really, Kate," faltered Philip, "I can't——"

"Give it to me, then," said Kate.

She was tugging with her trembling hand at the arm of the apple-tree, and the white blossom was raining over her from the rowels of the thin boughs overhead, like silver fish falling from the herring-net. Taking the letter, she glanced over the close—

"darlin Kirry how is the mackral this saison and is the millin doing middling and I wonder is the hens all layin and is the grace gone out of the mares leg yet and how is the owl man and is he still playin hang with the texes. Theer is a big chap heer that is strait like him he hath swallowed the owl Book and cant help bring it up agen but dear Kirry no more at present i axpect to be Home sune bogh, to see u all tho I dont no azactly With luv your luving swateart peat."

When she had finished the letter, she turned it over in her fingers, and gave another patient little sigh. "You didn't read it as it was spelled, Philip," she said.

"What odds if the spelling is uncertain when the love is as sure as that?" said Philip.

"Did he write it himself, think you?" said Kate.

"He signed it, anyway, and no doubt indited it too; but perhaps one of the Gills boys held the pen."

She coloured a little, slipped the letter down her dress into her pocket, and looked ashamed.

VIII

This shame at Pete's letter tormented Philip, and he stayed away again. His absence stimulated Kate and made Philip himself ashamed. She was vexed with him that he did not see that all this matter of Pete was foolishness. It was absurd to think of a girl marrying a man whom she had known when he was a boy. But Philip was trying to keep the bond sacred, and so she made her terms with it. She used Pete as a link to hold Philip.

After the lapse of some months, in which Philip had not been seen at Sulby, she wrote him a letter. It was to say how anxious she had been at the length of time since she had last heard from Pete, and to ask if he had any news to relieve her fears. The poor little lie was written in a trembling hand which shook honestly enough, but from the torment of other feelings.

Philip answered the letter in person. Something had been speaking to him day and night, like the humming of a top, finding him pretexts on which to go; but now he had to make excuses for staying so long away. It was evening. Kate was milking, and he went out to her in the cowhouse.

"We began to think we were to see no more of you," she said, over the rattle of the milk in the pail.

"I've—I've been ill," said Philip.

The rattle died to a thin hiss. "Very ill?" she asked.

"Well, no—not seriously," he answered.

"I never once thought of that," she said. "Something ought to have told me. I've been reproaching you, too."

Philip felt shame of his subterfuge, but yet more ashamed of the truth; so he leaned against the door and watched in silence. The smell of hay floated down from the loft, and the odour of the cow's breath came in gusts as she turned her face about. Kate sat on the milking-stool close by the ewer, and her head, on which she wore a sun-bonnet, she leaned against the cow's side.

"No news of Pete, then? No?" she said.

"No," said Philip.

Kate dug her head deeper in the cow, and muttered, "Dear Pete! So simple, so natural."

"He is," said Philip.

"So good-hearted, too."

"Yes."

"And such a manly fellow—any girl might like him," said Kate.

"Indeed, yes," said Philip.

There was silence again, and two pigs which had been snoring on the manure heap outside began to snort their way home. Kate turned her head so that the crown of the sun-bonnet was toward Phillip, and said—

"Oh, dear! Can there be anything so terrible as marrying somebody you don't care for?"

"Nothing so bad," said Philip.

The mouth of the sun-bonnet came round. "Yes, there's one thing worse, Philip."

"No?"

"Not having married somebody you do," said Kate, and the milk rattled like hail.

In the straw behind. Kate there was a tailless Manx cat with three tailed kittens, and Philip began to play with them. Being back to back with Kate, he could keep his countenance.

"This old Horney is terrible for switching," said Kate, over her shoulder. "Don't you think you could hold her tail?"

That brought them face to face again. "It's so sweet to have some one to talk to about Pete," said Kate.

"Yes?"

"I don't know how I could bear his long absence but for that."

"Are you longing so much, Kate?"

"Oh, no, not longing—not to say longing. Only you can't think what it is to be... have you never been yourself, Philip?"

"What?" "Hold it tight... in love? No?"

"Well," said Philip, speaking at the crown of the sun-bonnet. "Ha! ha! well, not properly perhaps—I don't—I can hardly say, Kate."

"There! You've let it go, after all, and she's covered me with the milk! But I'm finished, anyway."

Kate was suddenly radiant. She kissed Horney, and hugged her calf in the adjoining stall; and as they crossed the haggard, Philip carrying the pail, she scattered great handfuls of oats to a cock and his two hens as they cackled their way to roost.

"You'll be sure to come again soon, Philip, eh? It's so sweet to have some one to remind me of— —" but Pete's name choked her now. "Not that I'm likely to forget him—now is that likely? But it's such a weary time to be left alone, and a girl gets longing. Did I now? Give me the milk, then. Did I say I wasn't? Well, you can't expect a girl to be *always* reasonable."

"Good-bye, Kate."

"Yes, you had better go now—good-bye."

Philip went away in pain, yet in delight, with a delicious thrill, and a sense of stifling hypocrisy. He had felt like a fool. Kate must have thought him one. But better she should think him a fool than a traitor. It was all his fault. Only for him the girl would have been walled round by her love for Pete. He would come no more.

IX

Philip held to his resolution for three months, and grew thin and pale. Then another letter came from Pete—a letter for himself, and he wondered what to do with it. To send it by post, pretending to be ill again, would be hypocrisy he could not support. He took it.

The family were all at home. Nancy had just finished a noisy churning, and Kate was in the dairy, weighing the butter into pounds and stamping it. Philip read the letter in a loud voice to the old people in the kitchen, and the soft thumping and watery swishing ceased in the damp place adjoining. Pete was in high feather. He had made a mortal lot of money lately, and was for coming home quickly. Couldn't say exactly when, for some rascally blackleg Boers, who had been corrupting his Kaffirs and slipped up country with a pile of stones, had first to be followed and caught. The job wouldn't take long though, and they might expect to see him back within a twelvemonth, with enough in his pocket to drive away the devil and the coroner anyway.

"Bould fellow!" said Cæsar.

"Aw, deed on Pete!" said Grannie.

"Now, if it wasn't for that Ross— —" said Nancy.

Philip went into the dairy, where Kate was now skimming the cream of the last night's milking. He was sorry there was nothing but a message for her this time. Had she answered Pete's former letters? No, she had not.

"I must be writing soon, I suppose," she said, blowing the yellow surface. "But I wish—*puff*—I could have something to tell him—*puff, puff*—about you."

"About me, Kate?"

"Something sweet, I mean "—*puff, puff, puff*.

She shot a sly look upward. "Aren't you sure yet? Can't say still? Not properly? No?"

Philip pretended not to understand. Kate's laugh echoed in the empty cream tins. "How you want people to say things!"

"No, really—" began Philip.

"I've always heard that the girls of Douglas are so beautiful. You must see so many now. Oh, it would be delicious to write a long story to Pete. Where you met—in church, naturally. What she's like—fair, of course. And—and all about it, you know."

"That's a story you will never tell to Pete, Kate," said Philip.

"No, never," said Kate quite as light, and this being just what she wished to hear, she added mournfully. "Don't say that, though. You can't think what pleasure you are denying me, and yourself, too. Take some poor girl to your heart, Philip. You don't know how happy it will make you."

"Are *you* so happy, then, Kate?"

Kate laughed merrily. "Why, what do *you* think?"

"Dear old Pete—how happy *he* should be," said Philip.

Kate began to hate the very name of Pete. She grew angry with Philip also. Why couldn't he guess? Concealment was eating her heart out. The next time she saw Philip, he passed her in the market-place on the market-day, as she stood by the tipped-up gig, selling her butter. There was a chatter of girls all round as he bowed and went on. This vexed her, and she sold out at a penny a pound less, got the horse from the "Saddle," and drove home early.

On the way to Sulby she overtook Philip and drew up. He was walking to Kirk Michael to visit the old Deemster, who was ill. Would he not take a lift? He hesitated, half declined, and then got into the gig. As she settled herself comfortably after this change, he trod on the edge of her dress. At that he drew quickly away as if he had trodden on her foot.

She laughed, but she was vexed; and when he got down at "The Manx Fairy," saying he might call on his way back in the evening, she had no doubt Grannie would be glad to see him.

The girls of the market-place were standing by the mill-pond, work done, and arms crossed under their aprons, twittering like the pairing birds about them in the trees, when Philip returned home by Sulby. He saw Kate coming down the glen road, driving two heifers with a cushag for switch and flashing its gold at them in the horizontal gleams of sunset. She had recovered her good-humour, and was swinging along, singing merry snatches as she came—all life, all girlish blood and beauty.

She pretended not to see him until they were abreast, and the heifers were going into the yard. Then she said, "I've written and told him."

"What?" said Philip.

"That you say you are a confirmed old bachelor."

"That *I* say so?"

"Yes; and that *I* say you are so distant with a girl that I don't believe you have a heart at all."

"You don't?"

"No; and that he couldn't have left anybody better to look after me all these years, because you haven't eyes or ears or a thought for any living creature except himself."

"You've never written that to Pete?" said Philip.

"Haven't I, though?" said Kate, and she tripped off on tiptoe.

He tripped after her. She ran into the yard. He ran also. She opened the gate of the orchard, slipped through, and made for the door of the dairy, and there he caught her by the waist.

"Never, you rogue! Say no, say no!" he panted.

"No," she whispered, turning up her lips for a kiss.

X

Grannie saw nothing of Philip that night. He went home tingling with pleasure, and yet overwhelmed with shame. Sometimes he told himself that he was no better than a Judas, and sometimes that Pete might never come back. The second thought rose oftenest. It crossed his mind like a ghostly gleam. He half wished to believe it. When he counted up the odds against Pete's return, his pulse beat quick. Then he hated himself. He was in torment. But under his distracted heart there was a little chick of frightened joy, like a young cuckoo hatched in a wagtail's nest.

After many days, in which no further news had come from Pete, Kate received this brief letter from Philip:

"I am coming to see you this evening. Have something of grave importance to tell you."

It was afternoon, and Kate ran upstairs, hurried on her best frock, and came down to help Nancy to gather apples in the orchard. Black Tom was there, new thatching the back of the house, and Cæsar was making sugganes (straw rope) for him with a twister. There was a soft feel of autumn in the air, pigeons were cooing in the ledges of the mill-house gable, and everything was luminous and tranquil. Kate had climbed to the fork of a tree, and was throwing apples into Nancy's apron, when the orchard gate clicked, and she uttered a little cry of joy unawares as Philip entered. To cover this, she pretended to be falling, and he ran to help her.

"Oh, it's nothing," she said. "I thought the bough was breaking. So it's you!" Then, in a clear voice, "Is your apron full, Nancy? Yes? Bring another basket, then; the white one with the handles. Did you come Laxey way by the coach? Bode over, eh? Nancy, do you really think we'll have sugar enough for all these Keswicks?"

"Good evenin', Mr. Christian, sir," said Cæsar. And Black Tom, from the ladder on the roof, nodded his wide straw brim.

"Thatching afresh, Mr. Cregeen?"

"Covering it up, sir; covering it up. May the Lord cover our sins up likewise, or how shall we cover ourselves from His avenging wrath?"

"How vexing!" said Kate, from the tree. "Half of them get bruised, and will be good for nothing but preserving. They drop at the first touch—so ripe, you see."

"May we all be ripe for the great gathering, and good for preserving, too," said Cæsar. "Look at that big one, now—knotted like a blacksmith's muscles, but it'll go rotten as fast as the least lil one of the lot. It's taiching us a lesson, sir, that we all do fall—big mountains as aisy as lil cocks. This world is changeable."

Philip was not listening, but looking up at Kate, with a face of half-frightened tenderness.

"Do you know," she said, "I was afraid you must be ill again—your apron, Nancy—that was foolish, wasn't it?"

"No; *I* have been well enough," said Philip.

Kate looked at him. "Is it somebody else?" she said. "I got your letter."

"Can I help?" said Philip. "What is it? I'm sure there's something," said Kate.

"Set your foot here," he said.

"Let me down, I feel giddy."

"Slowly, then. Hold by this one. Give me your hand."

Their fingers touched, and communicated fire.

"Why don't you tell me?" she said, with a passionate tightening of his hand. "It's bad news, isn't it? Are you going away?"

"Somebody who went away will never come back," he answered.

"Is it—Pete?"

"Poor Pete is gone," said Philip.

Her throat fluttered. "Gone?"

"He is dead," said Philip.

She tottered, but drew herself up quickly. "Stop!" she said. "Let me make sure. Is there no mistake? Is it true?"

"Too true."

"I can bear the truth now—but afterwards—to-night—tomorrow—in the morning it might kill me if——"

"Pete is dead, Kate; he died at Kimberley."

"Philip!"

She burst into a wild fit of hysterical weeping, and buried her face his his breast.

He put his arms about her, thinking to soothe her. "There! be brave! Hold yourself firm. It's a terrible blow. I was too sudden. My poor girl. My brave girl!"

She clung to him like a terrified child; the tears came from under her eyelids tightly closed; the flood-gates of four years' reserve went down in a moment, and she kissed him on the lips.

And, throbbing with bliss and a blessed relief from four years hypocrisy and treason, he kissed her back, and they smiled through their tears.

Poor Pete! Poor Pete! Poor Pete!

XI

At the sound of Kate's crying, Cæsar had thrown away the twister and come close to listen, and Black Tom had dropped from the thatch. Nancy ran back with the basket, and Grannie came hurrying from the house.

Cæsar lifted both hands solemnly. "Now, you that are women, control yourselves," said he, "and listen while I spake. Peter Quilliam's dead in Kimberley."

"Goodness mercy!" cried Grannie.

"Lord alive!" cried Nancy.

And the two women went indoors, threw their aprons over their heads, and rocked themselves in their seats.

"Aw boy veen! boy veen!"

Kate came tottering in, ghostly white, and the women fell to comforting her, thereby making more tumult with their soothing moans than Kate with her crying.

"Chut'! Put a good face on it, woman," said Black Tom. "A whippa of a girl like you will be getting another soon, and singing, 'Hail, Smiling Morn!' with the best."

"Shame on you, man. Are you as drunk as Mackillya?" cried Nancy. "Your own grandson, too!"

"Never another for Kate, anyway," wept Grannie. "Aw boy veen, aw boy veen!"

"Maybe he had another himself, who knows?" said Black Tom. "Out of sight out of mind, and these sailor lads have a rag on lots of bushes."

Kate was helped to her room upstairs, Philip sat down in the kitchen, the news spread like a curragh fire, and the barroom was full in five minutes. In the midst of all stood Cæsar, solemn and expansive.

"He turned his herring yonder night when he left goodbye to the four of us," he said. "My father did the same the night he was lost running rum for Whitehaven, and I've never seen a man do it and live."

"It's forgot at you father," wept Grannie. "It was Mr. Philip that turned it. Aw boy veen! boy veen!"

"How could that be, mother?" said Cæsar. "Mr. Philip isn't dead."

But Grannie heard no more. She was busy with the consolations of half-a-dozen women who were gathered around her. "I dreamt it the night he sailed. I heard a cry, most terrible, I did. 'Father,' says I, 'what's that?' It was the same as if I had seen the poor boy coming to his end un-timeously. And I didn't get a wink on the night."

"Well, he has gone to the rest that remaineth," said Cæsar. "The grass perisheth, and the worm devoureth, and well all be in heaven with him soon."

"God forbid, father; don't talk of such dreadful things," said Grannie, napping her apron. "Do you say his mother, ma'am? Is she in life? No, but under the sod, I don't know the years. Information of the lungs, poor thing."

"I've known him since I was a slip of a boy," said one. "It was whip-top time—no, it was peg-top time——"

"I saw him the morning he sailed," said another. "I was standing *so*——"

"Mr. Christian saw him last," moaned Grannie, and the people in the bar-room peered through at Philip with awe.

"I felt like a father for the lad myself," said Cæsar, "he was always my white-headed boy, and I stuck to him with life. He desarved it, too. Maybe his birth was a bit mischancy, but what's the ould saying, 'Don't tell me what I was, tell me what I am.' And Pete was that civil with the tongue—a civiller young man never was."

Black Tom *tsht* and spat. "Why, you were shouting out of mercy at the lad, and knocking him about like putty. He wouldn't get lave to live with you, and that's why he went away."

"You're bad to forget, Thomas—I've always noticed it," said Cæsar.

"You'll be putting the bell about, and praiching his funeral, eh, Cæsar?" said somebody.

"'Deed, yes, man, Sabbath first," said Cæsar.

"That's impossible, father," said Grannie. "How's the girl to have her black ready?"

"Sunday week, then, or Sunday fortnight, or the Sunday after the Melliah (harvest-home)," said Cæsar; "the crops are waiting for saving, but a dead man is past it. Oh, I'll be faithful, I'll give it them straight, it's a time for spaking like a dying man to dying men; I'll take a tex' that'll be a lesson and a warning, 'Ho, every one that thirsteth— —"

Black Tom *tsht* and spat again. "I wouldn't, Cæsar; they'll think you're going to trate them," he muttered.

Philip was asked for particulars, and he brought out a letter. Jonaique Jelly, John the Clerk, and Johnny the Constable had come in by this time. "Read it, Jonaique," said Cæsar.

"A clane pipe first," said Black Tom. "Aren't you smook-ing on it, Cæsar? And isn't there a croppa of rum anywhere? No! Not so much as a plate of crackers and a drop of tay going? Is it to be a totaller's funeral then?"

"This is no time for feasting to the refreshment of our carnal bodies," said Cæsar severely. "It's a time for praise and prayer."

"I'll pud up a word or dwo," said the Constable meekly.

"Masther Niplightly," said Cæsar, "don't be too ready to show your gift. It's vanity. I'll engage in prayer myself." And Cæsar offered praise for all departed in faith and fear.

"Cæsar is nod a man of a liberal spirit, bud he is powerful in prayer, dough," whispered the Constable.

"He isn't a prodigal son, if that's what you mane," said Black Tom. "Never seen him shouting after anybody with a pint, anyway."

"Now for the letter, Jonaique," said Cæsar.

It was from one of the Gills' boys who had sailed with Pete, and hitherto served as his letter-writer.

"'Respected Sir,'" read Jonaique, "'with pain and sorrow I write these few lines, to tell you of poor Peter Quilliam— —'"

"Aw boy veen, boy veen!" broke in Grannie.

"'Knowing you were his friend in the old island, and the one he talked of mostly, except the girl— —'"

"Boy ve— —"

"Hush, woman."

"'He made good money out here, at the diamond mines— —'"

"Never a yellow sovereign he sent to me, then," said Black Tom, "nor the full of your fist of ha'pence either. What's the use of getting grand-childers?"

Cæsar waved his hand. "Go on, Jonaique. It's bad when the deceitfulness of riches is getting the better of a man."

"Where was I? Oh, 'good money ———' 'Yet he was never for taking joy in it——'"

"More money, more cares," muttered Cæsar.

"'But talking and talking, and scheming for ever, for coming home.'"

"Ah! home is a full cup," moaned Grannie. "It was a show the way that lad was fond of it. 'Give me a plate of mate, bolstered with cabbage, and what do I care for their buns and sarves, Grannie,' says he. Aw, boy veen, boy bogh!"

"What does the nightingale care for a golden cage when he can get a twig?" said Cæsar.

"Is the boy's chest home yet?" asked John the Clerk.

"There's something about it here," said Jonaique, "if people would only let a man get on."

"It's mine," said Black Tom.

"We'll think of that by-and-bye," said Cæsar, waving his hand to Jonaique.

"'He had packed his chest for going, when four blacklegs, who had been hanging round the compound, tempting and plaguing the Kaffirs, made off with a bag of stones. Desperate gang, too; so nobody was running to be sent after them. But poor Peter, being always a bit bull-necked, was up to the office in a jiffy, and Might he go? And off in chase in the everin' with the twenty Kaffirs of his own company to help him—not much of a lot neither, and suspected of dealing diamonds with the blacklegs times; but Peter always swore their love for him was getting thicker and stronger every day like sour cream. "The captain's love has been their theme, and shall be till they die," said Peter.'"

"He drank up the Word like a thirsty land the rain," said Cæsar. "Peter Quilliam and I had mortal joy of each other. 'Good-bye, father,' says he, and he was shaking me by the hand ter'ble. But go on, Jonaique."

"'That was four months ago, and a fortnight since eight of his Kaffirs came back.'"

"Aw dear!" "Well, well!" "Lord-a-massy!" "Hush!"

"'They overtook the blacklegs far up country, and Peter tackled them. But they had Winchester repeaters, and Peter's boys didn't know the muzzle of a gun from the neck of a gin-bottle. So the big man of the gang cocked his piece at Peter, and shouted at him like a high bailiff, "You'd better go back the way you came." "Not immajetly," said Peter, and stretched him. Then there was smoke like a smithy on hooping-day, and "To your heels, boys," shouted Peter. And if the boys couldn't equal Peter with their hands, they could bate him with their toes, and the last they heard of him he was racing behind them with the shots of the blacklegs behind him, and shouting mortal, "Oh, oh! All up! I'm done! Home and tell, boys! Oh, oh."'"

"Rejoice not against me, O mine enemy. When I fall I shall arise. Selah," said Cæsar.

Amid the tumult of moans which followed the reading, Philip, sitting with head on his hand by the ingle, grew hot and cold with the thought that after all there was no actual certainty that Pete was dead. Nobody had seen him die, nobody had buried him; the story of the returned Kaffirs might be a lie to cover their desertion of Pete, their betrayal of him, or their secret league with the thieving Boers. At one awful moment Philip asked himself how he had ever believed the letter. Perhaps he had *wanted* to believe it.

Nancy Joe touched him on the shoulder. "Kate is waiting for a word with you alone, sir," she said, and Philip crossed the kitchen into the little parlour beyond, chill with china and bowls of sea-eggs and stuffed sea-birds.

"He's feeling it bad," said Nancy.

"Never been the same since Pete went to the Cape," said Cæsar.

"I don't know for sure what good lads are going to it for," moaned Grannie. "And calling it Good Hope of all names! Died of a bullet in his head, too, aw dear, aw dear! Discussion of the brain it's like. And look at them black-heads too, as naked as my hand, I'll go bail. I hate the nasty dirts! Cæsar may talk of one flesh and brethren and all to that, but for my part I'm not used of black brothers, and as for black angels in heaven, it's ridiculous."

"When you're all done talking I'll finish the letter," said Jonaique.

"They can't help it, Mr. Jelly, the women can't help it," said Cæsar.

"'Respected Sir, I must now close, but we are strapping up the chest of the deceased, just as he left it, and sending it to catch the steamer, the *Johannesburg*, leaving Cape Town Wednesday fortnight——'"

"Hm! Johannesburg. I'll meet her at the quay—it's my duty to meet her," said Cæsar.

"And I'll board her in the bay," shouted Black Tom.

"Thomas Quilliam," said Cæsar, "it's borne in on my spirit that the devil of greed is let loose on you."

"Cæsar Cregeen, don't make a nose of wax of me," bawled Tom, "and don't think because you're praiching a bit that religion is going to die with you. Your head's swelling tre-menjous, and-you won't be able to sleep soon without somebody to tickle your feet. You'll be forgiving sins next, and taking money for absolution, and these ones will be making a pope of you and paying you pence. Pope Cæsar, the publican, in his chapel hat and white choker! But that chiss is mine, and if there's law in the land I'll have it."

With that Black Tom swept out of the house, and Cæsar wiped his eyes.

"No use smoothing a thistle, Mr. Cregeen," said Jonaique soothingly.

"I've a conscience void of offence." said Cæsar. "I can only follow the spirit's leading. But when Belial— —"

He was interrupted by a most mournful cry of "Look here! Aw, look, then, look!"

Nancy was coming out of the back-kitchen with something between the tips of her fingers. It was a pair of old shoes, covered with dirt and cobwebs.

"These were his wearing boots," she said, and she put them on the counter.

"Dear heart, yes, the very ones," said Grannie. "Poor boy, they'd move a heart of stone to see them. Something to remember him by, anyway. Many a mile his feet walked in them; but they're resting now in Abraham's bosom."

Then Cæsar's voice rose loud over the doleful tones around the counter. "'Vital Spark of Heavenly Flame'—raise it, Mr. Niplightly. Pity we haven't Peter and his fiddle here—he played with life."

"I can'd sing to-day, having a cold, bud I'll whisle id," said the Constable.

"Pitch it in altoes, then," said Cæsar. "I'm a bit of a base myself, but not near so base as Peter."

Meanwhile a little drama of serious interest was going on upstairs. There sat Kate before the looking-glass, with flushed cheeks and quivering mouth. The low drone of many voices came to her through the floor. Then a dull silence and one voice, and Nancy Joe coming and going between the kitchen and bedroom.

"What are they doing now, Nancy?" said Kate.

"First one's praying, and then another's praying," said Nancy. "Lord-a-massy, thinks I, it'll be my turn next, and what'll I say?"

"Where's Mr. Christian?"

"Gone into the parlour. I whispered him you wanted him alone."

"You never said that, Nancy," said Kate, at Nancy's reflection in the glass.

"Well, it popped out," said Nancy.

Kate went down, with a look of softened sorrow, and Philip, without lifting his eyes, began bemoaning Pete. They would never know his like—so simple, so true, so brave; never, never.

He was fighting against his shame at first seeing the girl after that kiss, which seemed to him now like treason at the mouth of a grave.

But, with the magic of a woman's art, Kate consoled him. He had one great comfort—he had been a loyal friend; such fidelity, such constancy, such affection, forgetting the difference of place, of education—everything.

Philip looked up at last, and there was the lovely face with its beaming eyes. He turned to go, and she said, softly, "How we shall miss you!"

"Why so?" said Philip.

"We can't expect to see you so often now—now that you've not the same reason for coming."

"I'll be here on Sunday," said Philip.

"Then you don't intend to desert us yet—not just yet, Philip?"

"Never!" said Philip.

"Well, good-night! Not that way—not by the porch. Good-night!"

As Philip went down the road in the darkness, he heard the words of the hymn that was being sung inside:

"Thy glory why didst Thou enshrine In such a clod of earth as mine, And wrap Thee in my clay."

XII

At that moment day was breaking over the plains of the Transvaal. The bare Veldt was opening out as the darkness receded, depth on depth, like the surface of an unbroken sea. Not a bush, not a path, only a few log-houses at long distances and wooden beacons like gibbets to define the Boer farms. No sound in the transparent air, no cloud in the unveiling sky; just the night creeping off in silence as if in fear of awakening the sleeping morning.

Across the soulless immensity a covered waggon toiled along with four horses rattling their link chains, and a lad sideways on the shaft dangling his legs, twiddling the rope reins and whistling. Inside the waggon, under a little window with its bit of muslin curtain, a man lay in the agony of a bullet-wound in his side, and an old Boer and a woman stood beside him. He was lying hard on the place of his pain and rambling in delirium.

"See, boys? Don't you see them?"

"See what, my lad?" said the Boer simply, and he looked through the waggon window.

"There's the head-gear of the mines. Look! the iron roofs are glittering. And yonder's the mine tailings. We'll be back in a jiffy. A taste of the whip, boys, and away!"

Untouched by visions, the old Boer could see nothing.

"What does he see, wife, think you?"

"What can he see, stupid, with his face in the pillow like that?"

With the rushing of blood in his ears the sick man called out again:

"Listen! Don't you hear it? That's the noise of the batteries. Whip up, and away! Away!" and he tore at the fringe of the blanket covering him with his unconscious fingers.

"Poor boy! he's eager to get to the coast But will he live to cover another morgen, think you?"

"God knows, Jan—God only knows."

And the Veldt was very wide, and the sea and its ships were far away, and over the weary stretch of grass, and rock, and sand, there was nothing on the horizon between desolate land and dominating sky but a waste looking like a chaos of purple and green, where no bird ever sang and no man ever lived, and God Himself was not.

XIII

"She loves me! She loves me! She loves me!" The words sang in Philip's ears like a sweet tune half the way back to Ballure. Then he began to pluck at the brambles by the wayside, to wound his hand by snatching at the gorse, and to despise himself for being glad when he should have been in grief. Still, he was sure of it; there was no making any less of it. She loved him, he was free to love her, there need be no hypocrisy and no self-denial; so he wiped the blood from his fingers, and crept into the blue room of Auntie Nan.

The old lady, in a dainty cap with flying streamers, was sitting by the fireside spinning. She had heard the news of Pete as Philip passed through to Sulby, and was now wondering if it was not her duty to acquaint Uncle Peter. The sweet and natty old gentlewoman, brought up in the odour of gentility, was thinking on the lines of poor Bridget, Black Tom when dying under the bare scraas, that a man's son was his son in spite of law or devil.

She decided against telling the Ballawhaine by remembering an incident in the life of his father. It was about Philip's father, too; so Philip stretched his legs from the sofa towards the hearth, and listened to the old Auntie's voice over the whirr of her wheel, with another voice—a younger voice, an unheard voice—breaking: in at the back of his ears when the wheel stopped, and a sweet undersong inside of him always, saying, "Be sensible; there is no disloyalty; Pete is dead. Poor Pete! Poor old Pete!"

"Though he had cast your father off, Philip, for threatening to make your mother his wife, he never believed there was a parson on the island would dare to marry them against his wish."

"No, really?"

"No; and when Uncle Peter came in at dinner-time a week after and said, 'It's all over,' he said, 'No, sir, no,' and threw down his spoon in the plate, and the hot broth splashed on my hand, I remember. But Peter said, 'It's past praying for, sir,' and then grandfather cried, 'No, I tell you no.' 'But I tell you yes, sir,' said Peter. 'Maughold Church yesterday morning before service.' Then grandfather lost himself, and called Peter 'Liar,' and cried that your father couldn't do it. 'And, besides, he's my own son after all, and would not,' said grandfather. But I could see that he believed what Uncle Peter had told him, and, when Peter began to cry, he said, 'Forgive me, my boy; I'm your father for all, and I've a right to your forgiveness.' All the same, he wouldn't be satisfied until he had seen the register, and I had to go with him to the church."

"Poor old grandfather!"

"The vicar in those days was a little dotty man named Kissack, and it was the joy of his life to be always crushing and stifling somebody, because somebody was always depriving him of his rights or something."

"I remember him—the Cockatoo. His favourite text was, 'Jesus said, then follow Me,' only the people declared he always wanted to go first."

"Shocking, Philip. It was evening when we drove up to Maughold, and the little parson was by the Cross, ordering somebody with a cane. 'I am told you married my son yesterday; is it true?' said grandfather. 'Quite true,' said the vicar. 'By banns or special license?' grandfather asked. 'License, of course,' the vicar answered."

"Curt enough, any way."

"'Show me the register,' said grandfather, and his face twitched and his voice was thick. 'Can't you believe me?' said the vicar. 'The register,' said grandfather. Then the vicar turned the key in the church door and strutted up the aisle, humming something. I tried to keep grandfather back even then. 'What's the use?' I said, for I knew he was only fighting against belief. But, hat in hand, he followed to the Communion rail, and there the vicar laid the open book before him. Oh, Philip, shall I ever forget it? How it all comes back—the little dim church, the smell of damp and of velvet under the holland covers of the pulpit, and the empty place echoing. And grandfather fixed his glasses and leaned over the register, but he could see nothing—only blurr, blurr, blurr.

"'*You* look at it, child,' he said, over his shoulder. But I daren't face it; so he rubbed his glasses and leaned over the book again. Oh dear! he was like one who looks down the list of the slain for the name he prays he may not find. But the name was there, too surely: 'Thomas Wilson Christian... to Mona Crellin... signed Wm. Crellin and something Kissack.'"

Philip's breath came hot and fast.

"The little vicar was swinging his cane to and fro on the other side of the rail and smiling, and grandfather raised his eyes to him and said, 'Do you know what you've done, sir? You've robbed me of my first-born son and ruined him.' 'Nonsense, sir,' said the vicar. 'Your son was of age, and his wife had the sanction of her father. Was I to go round by Ballawhaine for permission to do my duty as a clergyman?' 'Duty!' cried grandfather. 'When a young man marries, he marries for heaven or for hell. Your duty as a clergyman!' he cried, till his voice rang in the roof. 'If a son of yours had his hand at his throat, would you call it my duty as Deemster to hand him a knife.' 'Silence, sir,' said the vicar. Remember where you stand, or, Deemster though you are, you shall repent it.' 'Arrest me for brawling, will you?' cried grandfather, and he snatched the cane out of the vicar's hand and struck him across the breast. 'Arrest me now,' he said, and then tottered and stumbled out of the church by my arm and the doors of the empty pews."

Philip went to bed that night with burning brow and throbbing throat. He had made a startling discovery. He was standing where his father had stood before him; he was doing what his father had done; he was in danger of his father's fate! Where was his head that he had never thought of this before?

It was hard—it was terrible. Now that he was free to love the girl, he realised what it meant to love her. Nevertheless he was young, and he rebelled, he fought, he would not deliberate, The girl conquered in his heart that night, and he lay down to sleep.

But next morning he told himself, with a shudder, that it was lucky he had gone no farther. One step more and all the evil of his father's life might have been repeated in his own. There had been nothing said, nothing done. He would go to Sulby no more.

XIV

That mood lasted until mid-day, and then a scout of the line of love began to creep into his heart in disguise. He reminded himself that he had promised to go on Sunday, and that it would be unseemly to break off the acquaintance too suddenly, lest the simple folks should think he had borne with them throughout four years merely for the sake of Pete. But after Sunday he would take a new turn.

He found Kate dressed as she had never been before. Instead of the loose red bodice and the sun-bonnet, the apron and the kilted petticoat, she wore a close-fitting dark green frock with a lace collar. The change was simple, but it made all the difference. She was not more beautiful, but she was more like a lady.

It was Sunday evening, and the "Fairy" was closed. Csesar and Grannie were at the preaching-house, Nancy Joe was cooking crowdie for supper, and Kate and Philip talked. The girl was quieter than Philip had ever known her—more modest, more apt to blush, and with the old audacity of word and look quite gone. They talked of success in life, and she said—

"How I should like to fight my way in the world as you are doing! But a woman can do nothing to raise herself. Isn't it hard? Whatever the place where she was born in, she must remain there all her days. She can see her brothers rise, and her friends perhaps, but she must remain below. Isn't it a pity? It isn't that she wants to be rich or great. No, not that; only she doesn't want to be left behind by the people she likes. She must be, though, and just because she's a woman. I'm sure it's so in the Isle of Man, anyway. Isn't it cruel?"

"But aren't you forgetting something?" said Philip.

"Yes?"

"If a woman can't rise of herself because the doors of life are locked to her, it is always possible for a man to raise her."

"Some one who loves her, you mean, and so lifts her to his own level, and takes her up with him as he goes up?"

"Why not?" said Philip.

Kate's eyes beamed like sunshine. "That is lovely," she said in a low voice. "Do you know, I never thought of that before! If it were my case, I should like that best of all. Side by side with him, and he doing all? Oh, that is beautiful!"

And she gazed up with a timid joy at the inventive being who had thought of this as at something supernatural.

Cæsar and Grannie came back, both in fearful outbursts of Sunday clothes. Nevertheless Cæsar's eyes, after the first salutation with Philip, fixed themselves on Kate's unfamliar costume.

"Such worldly attire!" he muttered, following the girl round the kitchen and blowing up his black gloves. "This caring for the miserable body that will one day be lowered into the grave! What does the Book say?—put my tall hat on the clane laff, Nancy. 'Let it not be the outward adorning of putting on of apparel, but let it be the hidden man of the heart.'"

"But sakes alive, father," said Grannie, loosening a bonnet like a diver's helmet, "if it comes to that, what is Jeremiah saying, 'Can a maid forget her ornaments?'"

"It's like she can if she hasn't any to remember," said Cæsar. "But maybe the prophet Jeremiah didn't know the mothers that's in now."

"Chut, man! Girls are like birds, and the breed comes out in the feathers," said Grannie.

"Where's she getting it then? Not from me at all," said Cæsar.

"Deed, no, man," laughed Grannie, "considering the smart she is and the rasonable good-looking."

"Hould your tongue, woman; it'll become you better," said Cæsar.

Philip rose to go. "You're time enough yet, sir," cried Cæsar. "I was for telling you of a job."

Some of the fishermen of Ramsey had been over on Saturday. Their season was a failure, and they were loud in their protests against the trawlers who were destroying the spawn. Cæsar had suggested a conference at his house on the following Saturday of Ramsey men and Peel men, and recommended Philip as an advocate to advise with them as to the best means to put a stop to the enemies of the herring. Philip promised to be there, and then went home to Auntie Nan.

He told himself on the way that Kate was completely above her surroundings, and capable of becoming as absolute a lady as ever lived on the island, without a sign of her origin in look or speech, except perhaps the rising inflexion in her voice which made the talk of the true Manxwoman the sweetest thing in the world to listen to.

Auntie Nan was sitting by the lamp, reading her chapter before going to bed.

"Auntie," said Philip, "don't you think the tragedy in the life of father was accidental? Due, I mean, to the particular characters of grandfather and poor mother? Now, if the one had been less proud, less exclusive, or the other more capable of rising with her husband— —"

"The tragedy was deeper than that, dear; let me tell you a story," said Auntie Nan, laying down her book. "Three days after your father left Ballawhaine, old Maggie, the housemaid, came to my side at supper and whispered that some one was wanting me in the garden. It was Thomas. Oh dear! it was terrible to see him there, that ought to have been the heir of everything, standing like a stranger in the dark beyond the kitchen-door."

"Poor father!" said Philip.

"'Whist, girl, come out of the light,' he whispered. 'There's a purse with twenty pounds odd in my desk upstairs; get it, Nan, here's the key.' I knew what he wanted the money for, but I couldn't help it; I got him the purse and put ten pounds more of my own in it. 'Must you do it?' I said. 'I must,' he answered. 'Your father says everybody will despise you for this marriage,' I said. 'Better they should than I should despise myself,' said he. 'But he calls it moral suicide,' I said. 'That's not so bad as moral murder,' he replied. 'He knows the island,' I urged, 'and so do you, Tom, and so do I, and nobody can hold up his head in a little place like this after a marriage like that.' 'All the worse for the place,' said he, 'if it stains a man's honour for acting honourably.'"

"Father was an upright man," interrupted Philip. "There's no question about it, my father was a gentleman."

"'She must be a sweet, good girl, and worthy of you, or you wouldn't marry her,' said I to father; 'but are you sure that you will be happy and make her happy?' We shall have each other, and it is our own affair,' said father."

"Precisely," said Philip.

"'But if there is a difference between you now,' I said, 'will it be less when you are the great man we hope to see you some day?' 'A man is not always thinking of success,' he answered.

"My father was a great man already, Auntie," burst out Philip.

"He was shaken and I was ashamed, but I could not help it, I went on. 'Has the marriage gone too far?' I asked. 'It has never been mentioned between us,' said he. 'Your father is old, and can't live long,' I pleaded. 'He wants me to behave like a scoundrel,' he answered. 'Why that, if the girl has no right to you yet?' I said, and he was silent. Then I crept up and looked in at the window. 'See,' I whispered, 'he's in the library. We'll take him by surprise. Come!' It was not to be. There was a smell of tobacco on the air and the thud of a step on the grass. 'Who's that?' I said. 'Who should it be,' cried father, 'but the same spy again. I'll shake the life out of him yet as a terrier would a rat. No use, girl,' he shouted hoarsely, facing towards the darkness, 'they're driving me to destruction.' 'Hush!' I said, and covered his mouth with my hands, and his breath was hot, like fire. But it was useless. He was married three days afterwards."

Philip resolved to see Kate no more. He must go to Sulby on Saturday to meet the fishermen, but that would be a business visit; he need not prolong it into a friendly one. All the week through he felt as if his heart would break; but he resolved to conquer his feelings. He pitied himself somewhat, and that helped him to rise above his error.

XV

On Saturday night he was early at Sulby. The bat-room was thronged with fishermen in guernseys, sea-boots, and sou'-westers. They were all on their feet together, twisting about like great congers on the quay, drinking a little and smoking a great deal, thumping the table, and all talking at once. "How've you done, Billy?"—"Enough to keep away the divil and the coroner, and that's about all."—"Where's Tom Dug?"—"Gone to Austrilla."—"Is Jimmy over to-day?"—"He's away to Cleveland."—"Gough, bless me, every Manx boy seems to be going foreign."—"That's where we'll all be after long and last, if we don't stop these southside trawlers."

Philip went in and was received with goodwill and rough courtesy, but no man abated a jot of his freedom of action or liberty of speech, and the thumping and shouting were as loud as before. "Appeal to the Receiver-General."—"Chut! an ould woman with a face winking at you like a roast potato."—"Will we go to the Bishop, then?"—"A whitewashed Methodist with a soul the size of a dried pea."—"The Governor is the proper person," said Philip above the hubbub, "and he is to visit Peel Castle next Saturday afternoon about the restorations. Let every Manx fisherman who thinks the trawl-boats are enemies of the fish be there that day. Then lay your complaint before the man whose duty it is to inquire into all such grievances; and if you want a spokesman, I'm ready to speak for you."—"Bravo!"—"That's the ticket!"

Then the meeting was at an end; the men went on with stories of the week's fishing, stories of smugglers, stories of the Swaddlers (the Wesleyans), stories of the totalers (teetotallers), and Philip made for the door. When he got there, he began to reflect that, being in the house, he ought to leave good-night with Cæsar and Grannie. Hardly decent not to do so. No use hurting people's feelings. Might as well be civil. Cost nothing anyway. Thus an overpowering compulsion in the disguise of courtesy drew him again into Kate's company; but to-morrow he would take a new turn.

"Proud to see you, Mr. Philip," said Cæsar.

"The water's playing in the kettle; make Mr. Philip a cup of tay, Nancy," said Grannie. Cæsar was sitting back to the partition, pretending to read out of a big Bible on his knees, but listening with both ears and open mouth to the profane stories being told in the bar-room. Kate was not in the kitchen, but an open book, face downwards, lay on the chair by the turf closet.

"What's this?" said Philip. "A French exercise-book! Whoever can it belong to here?"

"Aw, Kirry, of coorse," said Grannie, "and sticking that close to it of an everin that you haven't a chance to put a word on her."

"Vanity, sir, vanity, all vanity," said Cæsar; and again he listened hard.

Philip's eyes began to blink. "Teaching herself French, is she? Has she been doing it long, Grannie?"

"Long enough, sir, three years or better, since poor Pete went away maybe; and at the books for ever, grammars and tex' books, and I don't know what."

Cæsar, with his ear at the glass, made an impatient gesture for silence, but Grannie continued, "I don't know what for people should be larning themselves foreign languages at all. For my part, there isn't one of them bates the Manx itself for plainness. And aren't we reading, when the Lord wanted to bring confusion on Noah and his disobedient sons and grandsons at going up the Tower of Babel, he made them spake different tongues?"

"Good thing too," snapped Cæsar, "if every poor man was bound to carry his wife up with him."

Philip's eyes were streaming, and, unobserved, he put the lesson-book to his lips. He had guessed its secret. The girl was making herself worthy of him. God bless, her!

Kate came downstairs in the dark dress and white collar of Sunday night. She saw Philip putting down the book, lowered her head and blushed, took up the volume, and smuggled it out of sight. Then Cæsar's curiosity conquered his propriety and he ventured into the bar-room, Grannie came and went between the counter and the fishermen, Nancy clicked about from dairy to door, and Kate and Philip were left alone.

"You were wrong the other night," she said. "I have been thinking it over, and you were quite, quite wrong."

"So?"

"If a man marries a woman beneath him, he stoops to her, and to stoop to her is to pity her, and to pity her is to be ashamed of her, and to be ashamed of her would kill her. So you are wrong."

"Yes?" said Philip.

"Yes," said Kate, "but do you know what it ought to be? The *woman* ought to marry beneath herself, and the man *above* himself; then as much as the woman descends, the man rises, and so— —-don't you see?"

She faltered and stopped, and Philip said, "Aren't you talking nonsense,' Kate?"

"Indeed, sir!"

Kate pretended to be angry at the rebuff, and pouted her lips, but her eyes were beaming.

"There is neither above nor below where there is real liking," said Philip. "If you like any one, and she is necessary to your life, that is the sign of your natural equality. It is God's sign, and all the rest is only man's book-keeping."

"You mean," said Kate, trying to keep a grave mouth, "you mean that if a woman belongs to some one she can like, and some one belongs to her, that is being equal, and everything else is nothing? Eh?"

"Why not?" said Philip.

It was music to her, but she wagged her head solemnly and said, "I'm sure you're wrong, Philip. I am, though. Yes, indeed I am. But it's no use arguing. Not against you. Only— —"

The glorious choir of love-birds in her bosom were singing so loud that she could say no more, and the irresistible one had his way. After a while, she stuffed something into the fire.

"What's that?" said Philip.

"Oh, nothing," she answered brightly.

It was the French exercise-book.

XVI

Philip went home rebelling against his father's fate. It was accidental; it was inevitable only in the Isle of Man. But perdition to the place where a man could not marry the woman he loved if she chanced to be born in the manger instead of the stable loft. Perdition to the land where a man could not live unless he was a skunk or a cur. Thank God the world was wide.

That night he said to Auntie Nan, "Auntie, why didn't father go away when he found the tide setting so strongly against him?"

"He always meant to, but he never could," said Auntie Nan. "A woman isn't like a man, ready to pitch her tent here to-day and there to-morrow. We're more like cats, dear, and cling to the places we're used to, if they're only ruins of tumbling stones. Your mother wasn't happy in the Isle of Man, but she wouldn't leave it. Your father wouldn't go without her, and then there was the child. He was here for weal or woe, for life or death. When he married his wife he made the chain that bound him to the island as to a rock."

"It wouldn't be like that with Kate," thought Philip. But did Auntie know anything? Had somebody told her? Was she warning him? On Sunday night, on the way home from church, she talked of his father again.

"He came to see at last that it wasn't altogether his own affair either," she said. "It was the night he died. Your mother had been unwell and father had sent for me. It was a dark night, and late, very late, and they brought me down the hill from Lewaige Cottage with a lantern. Father was sinking, but he *would* get out of bed. We were alone together then, he and I, except for you, and you were asleep in your cot by the window. He made straight for it, and struggled down on his knees at its side by help of the curtains. 'Listen,' he said, trying to whisper, though he could not, for his poor throat was making noises. You were catching your breath, as if sobbing in your sleep. 'Poor little boy, he's dreaming,' said I; 'let me turn him on his side.' 'It's not that,' said father; 'he went to sleep in trouble.'"

"I remember it, Auntie," said Philip. "Perhaps he had been trying to tell me something."

"'My boy, my son, forgive me, I have sinned against you,' he said, and he tried to reach over the cot rail and put his lips to your forehead, but his poor head shook like palsy and bobbed down into your little face. I remember you rubbed your nose with your little fist, but you did not waken. Then I helped him back to bed, and the table with the medicine glasses jingled by the trembling of his other hand. 'It's dark, all, all dark, Nannie,' he said, 'sure some angel will bring me light,' and I was so simple I thought he meant the lamp, for it was dying down, and I lit a candle."

Philip went about his work that week as if the spirit of his father were hovering over him, warning him when awake in words of love and pleading, crying to him in his sleep in tones of anger and command, "Stand back; you are at the edge of the precipice."

Nevertheless his soul rose in rebellion against this league as of the past and the dead. It was founded in vanity, in the desire for glory and success. Only let a man renounce the world and all that the world can give, and he can be true to himself, to his heart's impulse, to his honour, and to his love. He would deliberate no longer. He despised himself for deliberating. If was the world against Kate, let the world go to perdition.

XVII

On Saturday afternoon he was at Peel. It was a beautiful day; the sun was shining, and the bay was blue and flat and quiet. The tide was down, the harbour was empty of water, but full of smacks with hanging sails and hammocks of nets and lines of mollags (bladders) up to the mast heads. A flight of seagulls were fishing in the mud, and swirling through the brown wings of the boats and crying. A flag floated over the ruins of the castle, the church-bells were ringing, and the harbour-masters were abroad in best blue and gold buttons.

On the tilting-ground of the castle the fishermen had gathered, sixteen hundred strong. There were trawlers among them, Manx, Irish, and English, prowling through the crowd, and scooping up the odds and ends of gossip as their boats on the bottom scraped up the little fish. Occasionally they were observed by the herring-fishers, and then there were high words and free fights. "Taking a creep round from Port le Murrey are you, Dan?"—"Thought I'd put a sight on Peel to-day."—"Bad for your complexion, though; might turn it red, I'm thinking."—"Strek me with blood will you? I'd just like you to strek me, begough. I'd put a Union Jack on your face as big as a griddle."

The Governor came, an elderly man, with a formidable air, an aquiline nose, and cheeks pitted with small-pox. Philip introduced the fishermen and told their grievance. Trawling destroyed immature fish, and so contributed to the failure of the fisheries. They asked for power to stop it in the bays of the island, and within three miles of the coast.

"Then draft me a bill with that object, Mr. Christian," said the Governor, and the meeting ended with cheers for His Excellency, shouts for Philip, and mutterings of contempt from the trawlers. "Didn't think there was a man on the island could spake like it."—"But hasn't your fancy-man been rubbing his back agen the college?"—"I'd take lil tacks home if I was yourself, Dan."—"Drink much more and it'll be two feet deep inside of you."

Philip was hurrying away under the crumbling portcullis, when a deputation of the fishermen approached him. "What are we owing you, Mr. Christian?" asked their spokesman.

"Nothing," answered Philip.

"We thank you, sir, and you'll be hearing from us again. Meanwhile, a word if you plaze, sir?"

"What is it, men?" said Philip.

"When a young man can spake like yonder, it's a gift, sir, and he's houlding it in trust for something. The ould island's wanting a big man ter'ble bad, and it hasn't seen the like since the days of your own grandfather. Good everin, and thank you—good everin!"

With that the rough fellows dismissed him at the ferry steps, and he hastened to the market-place, where he had left his horse. On putting up, he had seen Cæsar's gig tipped up in the stable-yard. It was now gone, and, without asking questions, he mounted and made towards Ramsey.

He took the old road by the cliffs, and as he cantered and galloped, he hummed, and whistled, and sang, and slashed the trees to keep himself from thinking. At the crest of the hill he sighted the gig in front, and at Port Lady he came up with it. Kate was driving and Cæsar was nodding and dozing.

"You've been having a great day, Mr. Christian," said Cæsar. "Wish I could say the same for myself; but the heart of man is decaitful, sir, and desperately wicked. I'm not one to clap people in the castle and keep them from sea for debts of drink, and they're taking a mane advantage. Not a penny did I get to-day, sir, and many a yellow sovereign owing to me. If I was like some—now there's that Tom Raby, Glen Meay. He saw Dan the Spy coming from the total meeting last night. 'Taken the pledge, Dan?' says he. 'Yes, I have,' says Dan. 'I'm plazed to hear it,' says he; 'come in and I'll give you a good glass of rum for it.' And Dan took the rum for taking the pledge, and there he was as drunk as Mackilley in the castle this morning."

Philip listened as he rode, and a half-melancholy, half-mocking expression played on his face. He was thinking of his grandfather, old Iron Christian, brought into relation with his mother's father, Capt. Billy Ballure, of the dainty gentility of Auntie Nan and the unctuous vulgarity of the father of Kate.

Cæsar grumbled himself to sleep at last, and then Philip was alone with the girl, and riding on her side of the gig. She was quiet at first, but a joyous smile lit up her face.

"I was in the castle, too," she said, with a look of pride.

The sun went down over the waters behind them, and cast their brown shadows on the road in front; the twilight deepened, the night came down, the moon rose in their faces, and the stars appeared. They could hear the tramp of the horses' hoofs, the roll of the gig wheels, the wash and boom of the sea on their left, and the cry Of the sea-fowl somewhere beneath. The lovelinese and warmth of the autumn night stole over Kate, and she began to keep up a flow of merry chatter.

"I can tell all the sounds of the fields in the darkness. By the moonlight? No; but with my eyes shut, if you like. Now try me."

She closed her eyes and went on: "Do you hear that—that patter like soft rain? That's oats nearly ripe for harvest. Do you hear that, then—that pit-a-pat, like sheep going by on the street? That's wheat, just ready. And there—that whiss, whiss, whiss? That's barley."

She opened her eyes: "Don't you think I'm very clever?"

Philip felt an impulse to lean over the wheel and put his arms about the girl's neck.

"Take care," she cried merrily; "your horse is shying."

He gazed at her face, lit up in the white moonlight. "How bright and happy you seem, Kate!" he said with a shiver; and then he laid one hand on the gig rail.

Her eyelids quivered, her mouth twitched, and she answered gaily, "Why not? Aren't you? You ought to be, you know. How glorious to succeed? It means so much—new things to see, new houses to visit, new pleasures, new friends——"

Her joyous tones broke down in a nervous laugh at that last word, and he replied, in a faltering voice, "That may be true of the big world over yonder, Kate, but it isn't so in a little island like ours. To succeed here is like going up the tower of Castle Rushen with some one locking the doors on the stone steps behind you. At every storey the room becomes less, until at the top you have only space to stand alone. Then, if you should ever come down again, there's but one way for you—over the battlements with a crash."

She looked up at him with startled eyes, and his own were large and full of trouble. They were going through Kirk Michael by the house of the

Deemster, who was ill, and both drew rein and went slowly. Some acacias in the garden slashed their broadswords in the night air, and a windmill behind stood out against the moon like a gigantic bat. The black shadow of the horses stepped beside them.

"Are you feeling lonely to-night, Philip?"

"I'm feeling——"

"Yes?"

"I'm feeling as if the dead and the living, the living and the dead—oh, Kate, Kate, I don't know what I'm feeling."

She put her hand caressingly on the top of his hand. "Never mind, dear," she said softly; "I'll stand by you. You shan't be *alone*."

XVIII

It was midday, then, on the tropic seas, and the horizon was closing in with clouds as of blood and vapours of stifling heat. A steamship was rolling in a heavy swell, under winds that were as hot as gusts from an open furnace. Under its decks a man lay in an atmosphere of fever and the sickening odour of bandages and stale air. Above the throb of the engines and the rattle of the rudder chain he heard a step going by his open door, and he called in a feeble voice that was cheerful and almost merry, but yet the voice of a homesick boy—

"How many days from home, engineer?"

"Not more than twenty now."

"Put on steam, mate; put it on. Wish I could be skipping below and stoking up for you like mad."

As the ship rolled, the green reflection of the water and the red light of the sky shot alternately through the porthole and lit up the berth like firelight flashing in a dead house.

"Ask the boys if they'll carry me on deck, sir—just for a breath of fresh air."

The sailors came and carried him. "You can do anything for a chap like that."

The big sun was straight overhead, weighing down on their shoulders, and there was no shelter anywhere, for the shadows were under foot.

"Slip out the sails, lads, and let's fly along. Wish I could tumble up the rigging myself and look out from the yards same as a gull, but I'm only an ould parrot chained down to my stick."

They left him, and he gazed out on the circle of water and the vapour shaking over it like a veil. The palpitating air was making the circle smaller every minute, but the world seem cruelly large for all that. He was looking beyond the visible things; he was listening deeper than the wash of the waves; he was dreaming, dreaming. Apparitions were floating in the heat-clouds over him. Home! Its voices whispered at his ear, its face peered into his eyes. But the hot winds came up and danced round him; the air, the sea, the sky, the whole world, the utter universe seemed afire; his eyes rolled upwards to his brow; he almost choked and fainted.

"Carry him below, poor fellow! He's got a good heart to think he'll ever see home again. He'll never see it."

Half-way down the companion-ladder he opened his eyes with a look of despair. Would God let him die after all?

"Go on, girl. Does that twister want oiling? Feed it, woman, feed it," said Cæsar.

"His father should have been Dempster before him," said John, the clerk. "Would have been too, only he went crooked when he married on yonder woman. She's through though, and what more natural——"

The rope stopped again, and Kate's voice, hard and thick, came from the farther end of it. "His mother being dead, eh?"

"It was the mother that done for the father, anyway," said the clerk.

"Consequently," said Kate, "he is to praise God that his mother is gone!"

"That girl wants a doctor," muttered Jonaique.

"The man couldn't drag the woman up after him," began the clerk. "It's always the way——"

"Just that," said Kate, with bitter irony.

"Of coorse, I'm not for saying it was the woman's fault entirely——"

"Don't apologise for her," said Kate. "She's gone and forgotten, and that being so, her son has now a chance of being Deemster."

"So he has," shouted Cæsar, "and not second Dempster only, but first Dempster itself in time, and go on with the twister."

Kate laughed loudly, and cried, "Why don't you keep it up when your hand's in? First Deemster Christian, and then Sir Philip Christian, and then Lord Christian, and then——But you're talking nonsense, and you're a pack of tattlers. There's no thought of making Philip Christian a Deemster, and no hope of it and no chance of it, and I trust there never will be."

So saying, she flung the twister on the floor and rushed out of the mill, sobbing hysterically.

"Dr. Clucas is wonderful for females and young girls," said Jonaique.

"It's that Ross again," muttered Cæsar.

"And he'll have her yet," said Kelly, the postman.

"I'd see her dead first," said Cæsar. "It would be the jaws of hell and the mouth of Satan."

That she who loved Philip to distraction should be the first to abuse and defame him was agony near to madness, for Kate knew where she stood. It was not merely that Philip's success was separating them, not merely that the conventions of life, its usages, its manners, and its customs were putting worlds between them. The pathos of the girl's position was no accidental thing. It was a deeper, older matter; it was the same to-day as it had been yesterday and would be to-morrow; it began in the garden of Eden and would go on till the last woman died—-it was the natural inferiority of woman in relation to man.

She had the same passions as Philip, and was moved by the same love. But she was not free. Philip alone was free. She had to wait on Philip's will, on Philip's word. She saw Philip slipping away from her, but she could not snatch at him before he was gone; she could not speak first; she could not say, "I love you; stay with me!" She was a woman, only a woman! How wretched to be a woman! How cruel!

But ah! the dear delicious thought! It came stealing up into her heart when the red riot was nearly killing her. What a glorious thing it was to be a woman after all! What a powerful thing! What a lovely and beloved thing! To rule the king, being the slave, was sweeter than to be the king himself. That was woman's place. It was where heaven itself had put her from the beginning until now. What weapons had it given her! Beauty! Charm! Love! The joy of it! To be the weak and overcome the strong! To be nothing in the battle of life, and yet conqueror of all the world!

Kate vowed that, come what would, Philip should never leave her.

XX

On the day when the last of the harvest is saved in the Isle of Man, the farmer gives a supper to his farm-people, and to the neighbours who have helped him to cut and house it. This supper, attended by simple and beautiful ceremonies, is called the Melliah. The parson may be asked to it, and if there is a friend of position and free manners, he also is invited. Cæsar's Melliah fell within a week of the rope-making in the mill, and partly to punish Kate, partly to honour himself, he asked Philip to be present.

"He'll come," thought Kate with secret joy, "I'm sure he'll come;" and in this certainty, when the day of Melliah came, she went up to her room to dress for it. She was to win Philip that day or lose him for ever. It was to be her trial day—she knew that. She was to fight as for her life, and gain or lose everything. It was to be a battle royal between all the conventions of life, all the network of female custom, all the inferiority of a woman's position as God himself had suffered it to be, and one poor girl.

She began to cry, but struggling with her sadness, she dashed the tears from her glistening eyes. What was there to cry about? Philip *wanted* to love her, and he should, he must.

It was a glorious day, and not yet more than two o'clock. Nancy had washed up the dinner things, the fire-irons were polished, the boots and spare whips were put up on, the lath, the old hats like lines of heads on a city gate were hung round the kitchen walls, the hearthrug was down, the turf was piled up on the fire, the kettle was singing from the slowrie, and the whole house was taking its afternoon nap.

Kate's bedroom looked over the orchard and across the stackyard up the glen. She could see the barley stack growing in the haggard; the laden cart coming down the glen road with the driver three decks up over the mare, now half smothered and looking suddenly little, like a snail under the gigantic load; and beyond the long meadow and the Bishop's bridge, the busy fields dotted with the yellow stooks and their black shadows like a castle's studded doors.

When she had thrown off her blue-black dress to wash her arms and shoulders and neck were bare. She caught sight of herself in the glass, and laughed with delight. The years had brought her a fuller flow of life. She was beautiful, and she knew it. And Philip knew it too, but he should know it to day as he had never known it before. She folded her arms in their roundness over her bosom in its fulness and walked up and down the little room over the sheep-skin rugs, under the turfy scraas, glowing in the joy of blooming health and conscious loveliness. Then she began to dress.

She took from a drawer two pairs of stockings, one black and the other red, and weighed their merits with moral gravity—which? The red had it, and then came the turn of the boots. There was a grand new pair, with countless buttons, two toecaps like two flowers, and an upward curve like the arm of a glove. She tried them on, bent back and forward, but relinquished them with a sigh in favour of plain shoes cut under the ankles and tied with tape.

Her hair was a graver matter. Its tangled curls had never satisfied her. She tried all means to bring them into subjection; but the roll on top was ridiculous, and the roll behind was formal. She attempted long waves over the temples. It was impossible. With a lash-comb she dragged her hair back to its natural lawlessness, and when it fell on her forehead and over her ears and around her white neck in little knowing rings that came and went, and peeped out and slid back, like kittens at hide-and-seek, she laughed and was content.

From a recess covered by a shawl running on a string she took down her bodice. It was a pink blouse, loose over the breast, like hills of red sand on the shore, and loose, too, over the arms, but tight at the wrist. When she put it on it lit up her head like a gleam from the sunset, and her eyes danced with delight.

The skirt was a print, with a faint pink flower, the sash was a band of cotton of the colour of the bodice, and then came the solemn problems of the throat. It was round, and full, and soft, and like a tower. She would have loved to leave it bare, but dared not. Out of a drawer under the looking-glass she took a string of pearls. They were a present from Kimberley, and they hung over her fingers a moment and then slipped back. A white silk handkerchief, with a watermark, was chosen instead. She tied it in a sailor's knot, with the ends flying loose, and the triangular corner lying down her back.

Last of all, she took out of a box a broad white straw hat, like an oyster shell, with a silver-grey ribbon, and a sweeping ostrich feather.. She looked at it a moment, blew on it, plucked at its ribbon, lifted it over her head, held it at poise there, dropped it gently on to her hair, stood back from the glass to see it, and finally tore it off and sent it skimming on to the bed.

The substitute was her everyday sun-bonnet, which had been lying on the floor by the press. It was also of pale pink, with spots on its print like little shells on a big scallop. When she had tossed it over her black curls, leaving the strings to fall on her bosom, she could not help but laugh aloud.

After all, she was dressed exactly the same as on other days of life, except Sunday, only smarter, perhaps, and fresher maybe.

The sun-bonnet was right though, and she began to play with it. It was so full of play; it lent itself to so many moods. It could speak; it could say anything. She poked it to a point, as girls do when the sun is hot, by closing its mouth over the tip of her nose, leaving only a slumberous dark cave visible, through which her black eyes gleamed and her eyelashes shone. She tied the strings under her chin, and tipped the bonnet back on to her neck, as girls will when the breeze is cool, leaving her hair uncovered, her mouth twitching merrily, and her head like a nymph-head in an aureole. She took it off and tossed it on her arm, the strings still knotted, swinging it like a basket, then wafting it like a fan, and walking as she did so to and fro in the room, the floor creaking, her print frock crinkling, and she herself laughing with the thrill of passion vibrating and of imagined things to come.

Then she went downstairs with a firm and buoyant step, her fresh lithe figure aglow with young blood and bounding health.

At the gate of the "haggard" she met Nancy Joe coming out of the washhouse.

"Lord save us alive!" exclaimed Nancy. "If I ever wanted to be a man until this day!"

Kate kissed and hugged her, then fled away to the Melliah field.

XXI

Philip, in Douglas, had received the following communication from Government House:—

"His Excellency will be obliged to Mr. Philip Christian if he will not leave the island for the present without acquainting him of his destination."

The message was a simple one: it said little, and involved and foreshadowed nothing, but it threw Philip into a condition of great excitement. To relieve his restlessness by giving way to it, he went out to walk. It was the end of the tourist season, and the *Ben-my-Chree* was leaving the harbour. Newsboys, burrowing among the crowds on the pier to sell a Manx evening paper, were crying, "Illness of the Deemster—serious reports."

Philip's hair seemed to rise from his head. The two things came together in his mind. With an effort to smudge out the connection he turned back to his lodgings, looking at everything that his eyes fell on in the rattling streets, speaking to everybody he knew, but seeing nothing and hearing nobody. The beast of life had laid its claws on him.

Back in his rooms, he took out of his pocket a packet which Auntie Nan had put in his hand when he was leaving Ramsey. It was a bundle of his father's old letters to his sister cousin, written from London in the days when he was studying law and life was like the opening dawn. "The ink is yellow now," said Auntie Nan; "it was black then, and the hand that wrote them is cold. But the blood runs red in them yet. Read them, Philip," she said with a meaning look, and then he was sure she knew of Sulby.

Philip read his father's letters until it was far into the night, and he had gone through every line of them. They were as bright as sunshine, as free as air, easy, playful, forcible, full of picture, but, above all, egotistical, proud with the pride of intellectuality, and vain with the certainty of success. It was this egotism that fascinated Philip. He sniffed it up as a colt sniffs the sharp wind. There was no need to make allowances for it. The castles which his father had been building in the air were only as hovels to the golden palaces which his son's eager spirit was that night picturing. Philip devoured the letters. It was almost as if he had written them himself in some other state of being. The message from Government House lay on a table at his right, and sometimes he put his open hand over it as he sat close under the lamp on a table at his left and read on:—

... "Heard old Broom in the House last night, and today I lunched with him at Tabley's. They call him an orator and the king of conversationalists. He speaks like a pump, and talks like a bottle running water. No conviction, no sincerity, no appeal. Civil enough to me though, and when he heard that father was a Deemster, he told me the title meant Doomster, and then asked me if I knew the meaning of 'House of Keys,' and said it had its origin in the ancient Irish custom of locking the muniment chests with twenty-four keys, whereof each counsellor kept one. When he had left us Tabley asked if he wasn't a wonderful man, and if he didn't know something of everything, and I said, 'Yes, except the things of which I knew a little, and of them he knew nothing.'... My pen runs, runs. But, Nannie, my little Nannie, if this is what London calls a great man, I'll kick the ball like a toy before me yet."

... "So you are wondering where I am living—in man-sion or attic! Behold me then in Brick Court, Temple, second floor. Goldsmith wrote the 'Vicar' on the third, but I've not got up to that yet. His rooms were those immediately above me. I seem to see him coming down past my door in that wonderful plum-coloured coat. And sitting here at night I think of him—the sudden fear, the solitary death, then these stairs thronged with his pensioners, the mighty Burke pushing through, Reynolds with his ear-trumpet, and big 'blinking Sam,' and last of all the unknown grave, God knows where, by the chapel wall. Poor little Oliver! They say it was a women that was 'in' at the end. No more of the like now, no more debts, no more vain 'talk like poor Poll:' the light's out—all still and dark."

... "How's my little Nannie? Does she still keep a menagerie for sick dogs and lost cats? And how's the parson-gull with the broken wing, and does he still strut like Parson Kis-sack in his surplice? I was at Westminster Hall yesterday. It was the great trial of Mitchell, M. P., who forged his father's will. Stevens defended—bad, bad, bad, smirking all the while with small facetiæ. But Denman's summing up—oh! oh! such insight, such acuteness! It was wonderful. I had a seat in the gallery. The grand old hall was a thrilling scene—the dense throng, the upturned faces, the counsel, the judges, the officers of court, and then the windows, the statues, the echo of history that made every stone and rafter live—Oh, Nan, Nan, listen to me! If I live I'll sit on the bench there some day—I will, so help me God!"

When Philip had finished his father's letters, he was on the heights, and poor Kate was left far below, out of reach and out of sight. Hitherto his ambitions had been little more than the pale shadow of his father's hopes, but now they were his own realities.

XXII

Next morning the letter came from Cæsar inviting him to the Melliah, and then he thought of Kate more tenderly. She would suffer, she would cry—it would make his heart bleed to see her; but must he for a few tears put by the aims of a lifetime? If only Pete had been alive! If only Pete were yet to come home! He grew hot and ashamed when he remembered the time, so lately past, when the prayer of his secret heart would have been different. It was so easy now to hate himself for such evil impulses.

Philip decided to go to the Melliah. It would give him the chance he wanted of breaking off the friendship finally. More than friendship there had never been, except secretly, and that could not count. He knew he was deceiving himself; he felt an uneasy sense of loss of honour and a sharp pang of tender love as often as Kate's face rose up before him.

On the day of the Melliah he set off early, riding by way of St. John's that he might inquire at Kirk Michael about the Deemster.. He found the great man's house a desolate place. The gate was padlocked, and he had to clamber over it; the acacias slashed above him going down the path, and the fallen leaves encumbered his feet At the door, which was shut, he rang, and before it was opened to him an old woman put her untidy head out of a little window at the side.

"It's scandalous the doings that's here, sir," she whispered. "The Dempster's gone into 'sterics with the drink, and the lil farmer fellow, Billiam Cowley, is over and giving him as much as he wants, and driving everybody away."

"Can I speak to him?" said Philip.

"Billiam? It isn't fit. He'll blackguard you mortal, and the Dempster himself is past it. Just sitting with the brandy and drinking and drinking, and ateing nothing; but that dirt brought up on the Curragh shouting for beefstakes morning and night, and having his dinner laid on a beautiful new white sheet as clane as a bed."

From the ambush of a screen before an open door, Philip looked into the room where the Deemster was killing himself. The window shutters were up to keep out the daylight; candles were burning in the necks of bottles on the mantelpiece; a fire smouldered in a grate littered with paper and ashes; a coarse-featured man was eating ravenously at the table, a chop-bone in his fingers, and veins like cords moving on his low forehead—and the Deemster himself, judge of his island since the death of Iron Christian, was propped up in a chair, with a smoking glass on a stool beside him, and a monkey perched on his shoulder. "Turn them out, neck and crop, Dempster; the women are all for robbing a man," said the fellow; and a husky, eaten-out voice replied to him with a grunt and a laugh, "H'm! That's only what you're doing yourself, then, you rascal, and if I'd let the right one in long ago you wouldn't be here now—nor I neither, would I, Jacko?" The tail of the monkey flapped on the Deemster's breast, and Philip crept away with a shiver.

The sun was shining brightly outside the house, and the air was fresh and sweet. Remounting his horse, which was neighing and stamping at the gate, Philip rode hard to bring back a sense of warmth. At the "Fairy" he alighted and put up, and saw Grannie, who was laying tables in the mill.

"I'm busy as Trap's wife," she said, "and if you were the Govenar itself you wouldn't get lave to spake to me now. Put a sight on himself on the field yonder, the second meadow past the Bishop's bridge, and come back with the boys to supper."

Philip found the Melliah field. Two-score workers, men, women, and children, a cart and a pair of horses were scattered over it. Where the corn had been cut the day before the stubble had been woven overnight into a white carpet of cobwebs, which neither sun nor step of man had yet dispelled. There were the smell of the straw, the cawing of the rooks in the glen, the hissing to the breeze of the barley still standing, the swish of the scythe and the gling of the sickle, the bending and rising of the shearers, the swaying of the binders dragging the sheaves, the gluck of the wheels of the cart, the merry head of a child peeping out of a stook like a young bird out of the broken egg, and a girl in scarlet, whom Philip recognised, standing at the farthest hedge, and waving the corn band with which she was tieing to some one below.

Philip vaulted into the field, and was instantly seized by every woman working in it, except Kate, tied up with the straw ropes, and only liberated on paying the toll of an intruder.

"But I've come to work," he protested, and Cæsar who, was plotting the last rigs of the harvest, paired him with Kate and gave him a sickle. "He's a David, he'll smite down his thousands/," said Cæsar. Then cocking his eye up the field, "the Ballabeg for leader," he cried, "he's a plate-ribbed man. And let ould Maggie take the butt along with him. Jemmy the Red for the after-rig, and Robbie to follow Mollie with the cart Now ding-dong, boys, bend your backs and down with it."

Kate had not looked up when Philip came into the field, but she had seen him come, and she gave a little start when he took his place in his shirt-sleeves beside her. He used some conventional phrases which she scarcely answered, and then nothing was heard but the sounds of the sickle and the corn. She worked steadily for some time, and he looked up at her at intervals with her round bare arms and supple waist and firm-set foot and tight red stocking. Two butterflies tumbling in the air played around her sun bonnet and a lady-clock settled on her wrist.

Time was called for rest as Nancy Joe came through the gate bringing a basket with bottles and a can.

"The belly's a malefactor that forgets former kindness," said Cæsar; "ate and drink."

Then the men formed a group about the ale, the older women drank tea, the children making bands were given butter-milk, and the younger women with babes went cooing and clucking to the hedge where the little ones lay nuzzled up and unattended, some asleep in shawls, some awake on their backs and grabbing at the wondrous forests of marguerites towering up beside them, and all crying with one voice at sight of the breast, which the mothers were as glad to give as they to take.

The rooks cawed in the glen, there was a hot hum of bees, and a company of starlings passed overhead, glittering in the sunlight like the scales of a herring.

"They're taiching us a lesson," said Cæsar. "They're going together over the sea; but there's someones on earth would sooner go to heaven itself solitary, and take joy if they found themselves all alone and the cock of the walk there."

Kate and Philip stood and talked where they had been shearing quietly, simply, without apparent interest, and meanwhile the workers discussed them.

First the men: "He works his siggle like a man though."—"A stout boy anyway; give him practice and he'd shear many a man in bed." Then the women: "She's looking as bright as a pewter pot, and she's all so pretty as the Govenar's daughter too."—"Got a good heart, though. Only last week she had word of Pete, and look at the scarlet perricut." Finally both men and women: "Lave her alone, mother; it's that Ross that's wasting the woman."—"Well, if I was a man I'd know my tack."—"Wouldn't trust. It comes with Cæsar anyway; the Lord prospers him; she'll have her pickings.

Nothing bates religion in this world. It's like going to the shop with an ould Manx shilling—you get your pen'orth of taffy and twelve pence out."—"Lend's a hand with the jough then, boy. None left? Aw, Cæsar's wonderful religious, but there's never much lavings of ale with him."

Cæsar was striding through the stooks past Philip and Kate.

"Will it thrash well, Mr. Cregeen?" said Philip.

"Eight bolls to the acre maybe, but no straw to spake of, sir," said Cæsar. "Now, boys, let the weft rest on the last end, finish your work."

The workers fell to again, and the sickle of the leader sang round his head as he hacked and blew and sent off his breath in spits until the green grass springing up behind him left only a triangular corner of yellow corn. Fore-rig and the after-rig took a tussle together, and presently nothing was standing of all the harvest of Glenmooar but one small shaft of ears a yard wide or less. Then the leaders stopped, and all the shearers of the field came up and cast down their sickles into the soil in a close circle, making a sheaf of crescent moons.

"Now for the Melliah," said Cæsar. "Who's to be Queen?"

There was a cry for Kate, and she sailed forward buoyantly, fresh still, warm with her work, and looking like the afterglow from the sunset in the lengthening shadows from the west.

"Strike them from their legs, Kirry," cried Nancy Joe, and Kate drew up one of the sickles, swept her left arm over the standing corn, and at a single stroke of her right brought the last ears to the ground.

Then there was a great shout. "Hurrah for the Mel-liah!" It rang through the glen and echoed in the mountains. Grannie heard it in the valley, and said to herself, "Cæsar's Melliah's took."

"Well, we've gathered the ripe corn, praise His name," said Cæsar, "but what shall be done at the great gathering for unripe Christians?"

Kate lifted her last sheaf and tied it about with a piece of blue ribbon, and Philip plucked the cushag (the ragwort) from the hedge, and gave it her to put in the band.

This being done; the Queen of the Melliah stepped back, feeling Philip's eyes following her, while the oldest woman shearer came forward.

"I've a crown-piece, here that's being lying in my pocket long enough, Joney," said Cæsar with an expansive air, and he gave the woman her accustomed dole.

She was a timid, shrinking creature, having a face walled with wrinkles, and wearing a short blue petticoat, showing heavy dull boots like a man's, and thick black stockings.

Then the young fellows went racing over the field, vaulting the stooks, stretching a straw rope for the girls to jump over, heightening and tightening it to trip them up, and slacking and twirling it to make them skip. And the girls were falling with a laugh, and leaping up again and flying off like the dust, tearing their frocks and dropping their sun-bonnets as if the barley grains they had been reaping had got into their blood.

In the midst of this maddening frolic, while Cæsar and the others were kneeling behind the barley stack, Kate snatched Philip's hat from his head and shot like a gleam into the depths of the glen.

Philip dragged up his coat by one of its arms and fled after her.

XXIII

Sulby Glen is winding, soft, rich, sweet, and exquisitely beautiful. A thin thread of blue water, laughing, babbling, brawling, whooping, leaping, gliding, and stealing down from the mountains; great boulders worn smooth and ploughed hollow by the wash of ages; wet moss and lichen on the channel walls; deep, cool dubbs; tiny reefs; little cascades of boiling foam; lines of trees like sentinels on either side, making the light dim through the overshadowing leafage; gaunt trunks torn up by winds and thrown across the stream with their heads to the feet of their fellows; the golden fuschia here, the green trammon there; now and again a poor old tholthan, a roofless house, with grass growing on its kitchen floor; and over all the sun peering down with a hundred eyes into the dark and slumberous gloom, and the breeze singing somewhere up in the tree-tops to the voice of the river below.

Kate had run out on the stem of one of the fallen trees, and there Philip found her, over the middle of the stream, laughing, dancing, waving his hat in one hand, and making sweeping bows to her reflection in the water below.

"Come back," he cried. "You terrible girl, you'll fall. Sit down there—don't torment me, sit down."

After a curtsey to him she turned her attention to her skirts, wound them about her ankles, sat on the trunk, and dangled her shapely feet half an inch over the surface of the stream.

Then Philip had time to observe that the other end of the tree did not reach the opposite bank, but dipped short into the water. So he barricaded his end by sitting on it, and said triumphantly: "My hat, if you please."

Kate looked and gave a little cry of alarm and then a chuckle, and then she said—

"You thought you'd caught me, didn't you? You can't, though," and she dropped on to a boulder from which she might have skipped ashore.

"I can't, can't I?" said Philip; and he twisted a smaller boulder on his side, so that Kate was surrounded by water and cut off from the bank. "My hat now, madam," he said with majestic despotism. 10

She would not deliver it, so he pretended to leave her where she was. "Good-bye, then; good evening," he cried over the laughter of the stream, and turned away a step bareheaded.

A moment later his confidence was dashed. When he turned his head back Kate had whipped off her shoes and stockings, and was ramming the one inside the other.

"What are you doing?" cried Philip.

"Catch this—and this," she said, flinging the shoes across to him. Then clapping his straw hat on the crown of her sun-bonnet, she tucked up her skirts with both hands and waded ashore.

"What a clever boy you are! You thought you'd caught me again, didn't you?" she said.

"I've caught your shoes, anyway," said Philip, "and until you give me my hat I'll stick to them."

She was on the shingle, but in her bare feet, and could not make a step.

"My shoes, please?" she pleaded.

"My hat first," he answered.

"Take it."

"No; you must give it me."

"Never! I'll sit here all night first," said Kate.

"I'm willing," said Philip.

They were sitting thus, the one bare-headed, the other with bare feet, and on the same stone, as if seats in the glen were scarce, when there came the sound of a hymn from the field they had left, and then it was agreed by way of mutual penalty that Kate should put on Philip's hat on condition that Philip should be required to put on Kate's shoes.

At the next moment Philip, suddenly sobered, was reproaching himself fiercely. What was he doing? He had come to tell Kate that he should come no more, and this was how he had begun! Yesterday he was in Douglas reading his father's letters, and here he was to-day, forgetting himself, his aims in life, his duties, his obligations—everything. "Philip," he thought, "you are as weak as water. Give up your plans; you are not fit for them; abandon your hopes—they are too high for you."

"How solemn we are all at once!" said Kate.

The hymn (a most doleful strain, dragged out to death on every note) was still coming from the Melliah field, and she added, slyly, shyly, with a mixture of boldness and nervousness, "Do you think this world is so very bad, then?"

"Well—aw—no," he faltered, and looking up he met her eye, and they both laughed.

"It's all nonsense, isn't it?" she said, and they began to walk down the glen.

"But where are we going?"

"Oh, we'll come out this way just as well."

The scutch grass, the long rat-tail, and the golden cushag were swishing against his riding-breeches and her print dress. "I must tell her now," he thought. In the narrow places she went first, and he followed with a lagging step, trying to begin. "Better prepare her," he thought. But he could think of no commonplace leading up to what he wished to say.

Presently, through a tangle of wild fuchsia, there was a smell of burning turf in the air and the sound of milking into a pail, and then a voice came up surprisingly as from the ground, saying:

"Aisy on the thatch, Miss Cregeen, ma'am."

It was old Joney, the shearer, milking her goat, and Kate had stepped on to the roof of her house without knowing it, for the little place was low and opened from the water's edge and leaned against the bank.

Philip made some conventional inquiries, and she answered that she had been thirty years there, and had one son living with her, and he was an imbecile.

"There was once a flock at me, and I was as young as you are then, miss, and all as happy; but they're laving me one by one, except this one, and he isn't wise, poor boy."

Philip tried to steel his heart. "It is cruel," he thought, "it will hurt her; but what must be, must be." She began to sing and went carolling down the glen, keeping two paces in front of him. He followed like an assassin meditating the moment to strike. "He is going to say something," she thought, and then she sang louder.

"Kate," he called huskily.

But she only clapped her hands, and cried in a voice of delight, "The echo! Here's the echo! Let's shout to it."

Her kindling features banished his purpose for the time, and he delivered himself to her play. Then she called up the gill, "Ec—ho! Ec—ho!" and listened, but there was no response, and she said, "It won't answer to its own name. What shall I call?"

"Oh, anything," said Philip.

"Phil—ip! Phil—ip!" she called, and then said pettishly, "No, Philip won't hear me either." She laughed. "He's always so stupid though, and perhaps he's asleep."

"More this way," said Philip. "Try now."

"You try."

Philip took up the call. "Kate!" he shouted, and back came the answer, *Ate!* "Kate—y!"—*Ate—y*.

"Ah! how quick! Katey's a good girl. Hark how she answers you," said Kate.

They walked a few steps, and Kate called again, "Philip!" There was no answer. "Philip is stubborn; he won't have anything to do with me," said Kate.

Then Philip called a second time, "Katey!" And back came the echo as before. "Well, that's too bad. Katey is—yes, she's actually *following* you!"

Philip's courage oozed out of him. "Not yet," he thought. *Traa-dy-liooar*—time enough. "After supper, when everybody is going! Outside the mill, in the half light of candles within and darkness without! It will sound so ordinary then, 'Good-bye! Haven't you heard the news? Auntie Nan is reconciled at last to leaving Ballure and joining me in Douglas.' That's it; so simple, so commonplace."

The light was now coming between the trees on the closing west in long swords of sunset red. They could hear the jolting of the laden cart on its way down the glen. The birds were fairly rioting overhead, and all sorts of joyous sounds filled the air. Underfoot there were long ferns and gorse, which caught at her crinkling dress sometimes, and then he liberated her and they laughed. A trailing bough of deadly nightshade was hanging from the broken head of an old ash stump, whose wasted feet were overgrown by two scarlet-tipped toadstools, and she plucked a long tendril of it and wound it about her head, tipping her sun-bonnet back, and letting the red berries droop over her dark hair to her face. Then she began to sing,

O were I monarch o' the globe,
Wi' thee to reign, wi' thee to reign.

Radiant gleams shot out of her black pupils, and flashes of love like lightning passed from her eye to his.

Then he tried to moralise. "Ah!" he said, out of the gravity of his wisdom, "if one could only go on for ever like this, living from minute to minute! But that's the difference between a man and a woman. A woman lives in the world of her own heart. If she has interests, they centre there. But a man has his interests outside his affections. He is compelled to deny himself, to let the sweetest things go by."

Kate began to laugh, and Philip ended by laughing too.

"Look!" she cried, "only look."

On the top of the bank above them a goat was skirmishing. He was a ridiculous fellow; sometimes cropping with saucy jerks, then kicking up his heels, as if an invisible imp had pinched him, then wagging his rump and laughing in his nostrils.

"As I was saying," said Philip, "a man has to put by the pleasures of life. Now here's myself, for example. I am bound, do you know, by a kind of duty—a sort of vow made to the dead, I might say———"

"I'm sure he's going to say something," thought Kate. The voice of his heart was speaking louder and quicker than his halting tongue. She saw that a blow was coming, and looked about for the means to ward it off.

"The fairy's dubb!" she cried suddenly, and darted from his side to the water's edge.

It was a little round pool, black as ink, lying quiet and apparently motionless under a noisy place where the waters swirled and churned over black moss, and the stream ran into the dark. Philip had no choice but to follow her.

"Cut me a willow! Your penknife! Quick, sir, quick! Not that old branch—a sapling. There, that's it. Now you shall hear me tell my own fortune."

"An ordeal is it?" said Philip.

"Hush! Be quiet, still, or little Phonodoree wont listen. Hush, now hush!"

With solemn airs, but a certain sparkle in her eyes, she went down on her knees by the pool, stretched her round arm over the water, passed the willow bough slowly across its surface, and recited her incantation:

Willow bough, willow bough, which of the four,
Sink, circle, or swim, or come floating ashore?

Which is the fortune you keep for my life,
Old maid or young mistress or widow or wife?

With the last word she flung the willow bough on to the pool, and sat back on her heels to watch it as it moved slowly with the motion of the water.

"Bravo!" cried Philip.

"Be quiet. It's swimming. No, it's coming ashore."

"It's wife, Kate. No, it's widow. No, it's——"

"Do be serious. Oh, dear! it's going—yes, it's going round. Not that either. No, it has—yes, it has———oh!"

"Sunk!" said Philip, laughing and clapping his hands. "You're doomed to be an old maid, Kate. Phonodoree says so."

"Cruel Brownie! I'm vexed that I bothered with him," said Kate, dropping her lip. Then nodding to her reflection in the water where the willow bough had disappeared, she said, "Poor little Katey! He might have given you something else. Anything but that dear, eh?"

"What," laughed Philip, "crying? Because Phonodoree—never!"

Kate leapt up with averted face. "What nonsense you are talking!" she said.

"There are tears in your eyes, though," said Philip.

"No wonder, either. You're so ridiculous. And if I'm meant for an old maid, you're meant for an old bachelor—and quite right too!"

"Oh, it is, is it?"

"Yes, indeed. You've got no more heart than a mushroom, for you're all head and legs, and you're going to be just as bald some day."

"I am, am I, mistress?"

"If I were you, Philip, I should hire myself out for a scarecrow, and then having nothing under your clothes wouldn't so much matter."

"It wouldn't, wouldn't it?" said Philip.

She was shying off at a half circle; he was beating round her.

"But you're nearly as old as Methuselah already, and what you'll be when you're a man——"

"Lookout!"

She made him an arch curtsey and leapt round a tree, and cried from the other side, "I know. A squeaking old croaker, with the usual old song, 'Deed yes, friends, this world is a vale of sin and misery.' The men's the misery and the women's the sin——"

"You rogue, you!" cried Philip.

He made after her, and she fled, still speaking, "What do you think a girl wants with a——Oh! Oh! Oo!"

Her tirade ended suddenly. She had plunged into a bed of the prickly gorse, and was feeling in twenty places at once what it was to wear low shoes and thin stockings.

"With a Samson, eh?" cried Philip, striding on in his riding breeches, and lifting the captured creature in his arms. "Why, to carry her, you torment, to carry her through the gorse like this."

"Ah!" she said, turning her face over his shoulder, and tickling his neck with her breath.

Her hair caught in a tree, and fell in a dark shower over his breast. He set her on her feet; they took hands, and went carolling down the glen together:

"The brightest jewel in my crown, Wad be my queen, wad be my queen."

The daylight lingered as if loth to leave them. There was the fluttering of wings overhead, and sometimes the last piping of birds. The wind wandered away, and left their voices sovereign of all the air.

Then there came a distant shout; the cheer of the farm people on reaching home with the Melliah.. It awakened Philip as from a fit of intoxication.

"This is madness," he thought. "What am I doing?" "He is going to speak now," she told herself.

Her gaiety shaded off into melancholy, and her melancholy burst into wild gaiety again. The night had come down, the moon had risen, the stars had appeared. She crept closer to Philip's side, and began to tell him the story of a witch. They were near to the house the witch had lived in. There it was—that roofless cottage—that tholthan under the deep trees like a dungeon.

"Have you never heard of her, Philip? No? The one they called the Deemster's lady?"

"What Deemster?" said Philip.

"This one, Deemster Mylrea, who is said to be dying."

"He is dying; he is killing himself; I saw him to-day,' said Philip.

"'Well, she was the blacksmith's daughter, and he left her, and she went mad and cursed him, and said she was his wife though they hadn't been to church, and he should never marry anybody else. Then her father turned her out, and she came up here all alone, and there was a baby, and they were saying she killed it, and everybody was afraid of her. And all the time her boy was making himself a great, great man until he got to be Deemster. But he never married, never, though times and times people were putting this lady on him and then that; but when they told the witch, she only laughed and said, 'Let him, he'll get lave enough!' At last she was old and going on two sticks, and like to die any day, and then he crept out of his big house unknown to any one and stole up here to the woman's cottage. And when she saw the old man she said, 'So you've come at last, boy; but you've been keeping me long, bogh, you've been keeping me long.' And then she died. Wasn't that strange?"

Her dark eyes looked up at him and her mouth quivered.

"Was it witchcraft, then?" said Philip.

"Oh, no; it was only because he was her husband. That was the hold she had of him. He was tempted away by a big house and a big name, but he *had* to come back to her. And it's the same with a woman. Once a girl is the wife of somebody, she *must* cling to him, and if she is ever false she must return. Something compels her. That's if she's really his wife—really, truly. How beautiful, isn't it? Isn't it beautiful?"

"Do you think that, Kate? Do you think a man, like a woman, would cling the closer?"

"He couldn't help himself, Philip."

Philip tried to say it was only a girl's morality, but her confidence shamed him. She slipped her moist fingers into his hand again. They were close by the deserted tholthan, and she was creeping nearer and nearer to his side. A bat swirled above their heads and she made a faint cry. Then a cat shot from under a gooseberry bush, and she gave a little scream. She was breathing irregularly. He could smell the perfume of her fallen hair. He was in agony of pain and delight. His heart was leaping in his bosom; his eyes were burning.

"She's right," he thought. "Love is best. It is everything. It is the crown of life. Shall I give it up for the Dead Sea fruit of worldly success? Think of the Deemster! Wifeless, childless, living solitary, dying alone, unregretted, unmourned. What is the wickedness you are plotting? Your father is dead, you can do him neither good nor harm. This girl is alive. She loves you. Love her. Let the canting hypocrites prate as they will."

She had disengaged her hand, and was creeping away from him in the half darkness, treading softly and going off like a gleam.

"Kate!" he called.

He heard her laughter, he heard the drowsy hum of the gill, he could smell the warm odour of the gorse bushes.

"But this is madness," he thought. "This is the fever of an hour. Yield now and I am ruined for life. The girl has come between me and my aims, my vows, my work—everything. She has tempted me, and I am as weak as water."

"Kate!"

She did not answer.

"Come here this moment, Kate. I have something to say to you."

"Bite!" she said, coming back and holding an apple to his lips. She had plucked it in the overgrown garden.

"Listen! I'm leaving Ramsey for good—don't intend to practise in the northern courts any longer—settling in Douglas—best work lies there, you see—worst of it is—we shan't meet again soon—not very soon, you know—not for years, perhaps——"

He began by stammering, and went on stuttering, blurting out his words, and trembling at the sound of his own voice.

"Philip, you must not go!" she cried. "I'm sorry, Kate, very sorry. Shall always remember so tenderly—not to say fondly—the happy boy and girl days together."

"Philip, Philip, you must not go—you cannot go—you shall not go!"

He could see her bosom heaving under her loose red bodice. She took hold of his arm and dragged at it.

"Won't you spare me? Will you shame me to death? Must I tell you? If you won't speak, I will. You cannot leave me, Philip, because—because—what do I care?—because I love you!"

"Don't say that, Kate!"

"I love you, Philip—I love you—I love you!"

"Would to God I had never been born!"

"But I will show you how sweet it is to be alive. Take me, take me—I am yours!"

Her upturned face seemed to flash. He staggered like one seized with giddiness. It was a thing of terror to behold her. Still he struggled. "Though apart, we shall remember each other, Kate."

"I don't want to remember. I want to have you with me."

"Our hearts will always be together."

"Come to me then, Philip, come to me!"

"The purest part of our hearts—our souls——"

"But I want *you!* Will you drive a girl to shame herself again? I want *you*, Philip! I want your eyes that I may see them every day; and your hair, that I may feel it with my hands; and your lips—can I help it?—yes, and your lips, that I may kiss and kiss them!"

"Kate! Kate! Turn your eyes away. Don't look at me like that!" She was fighting for her life. It was to be now or never.

"If you won't come to me, I'll go to you!" she cried; and then she sprang upon him, and all grew confused, the berries of the nightshade whipped his forehead, and the moon and the stars went out.

"My love! My darling! My girl!"

"You won't go now?" she sobbed.

"God forgive me, I cannot."

"Kiss me. I feel your heart beating. You are mine—mine—mine! Say you won't go now!"

"God forgive us both!"

"Kiss me again, Philip! Don't despise me that I love you better than myself!"

She was weeping, she was laughing, her heart was throbbing up to her throat. At the next moment she had broken from his embrace and was gone.

"Kate! Kate!"

Her voice came from the tholthan.

"Philip!"

When a good woman falls from honour, is it merely that she is a victim of momentary intoxication, of stress of passion, of the fever of instinct? No. It is mainly that she is a slave of the sweetest, tenderest, most spiritual and pathetic of all human fallacies—the fallacy that by giving herself to the man she loves she attaches him to herself for ever. This is the real betrayer of nearly all good women that are betrayed. It lies at the root of tens of thousands of the cases that make up the merciless story of man's sin and woman's weakness. Alas! it is only the woman who clings the closer. The impulse of the man is to draw apart. He must conquer it or she is lost. Such is the old cruel difference and inequality of man and woman as nature made them—the old trick, the old tragedy.

XXIV

Old Mannanin, the magician, according to his wont, had surrounded his island with mist that day, and, in the helpless void of things unrevealed, a steamship bound for Liverpool came with engines slacked some points north of her course, blowing her fog-horn over the breathless sea with that unearthly yell which must surely be the sound whereby the devil summons his legions out of chaos.

Presently something dropping through the dense air settled for a moment on the damp rope of the companion ladder, and one of the passengers recognised it.

"My gough! It's a bird, a sparrow," he cried.

At the same moment there was a rustle of wind, the mist lifted, and a great round shoulder rose through the white gauze, as if it had been the ghost of a mountain.

"That's the Isle of Man," the passenger shouted, and there was a cry of incredulity. "It's the Calf, I'm telling you, boys. Lave it to me to know." And instantly the engines were reversed.

The passenger, a stalwart fellow, with a look as of pallor under a tawny tan, walked the deck in a fever of excitement, sometimes shouting in a cracked voice, sometimes laughing huskily, and at last breaking down in a hoarse gurgle like a sob.

"Can't you put me ashore, capt'n?"

"Sorry I can't, sir, we've lost time already."

There was a dog with him, a little, misshapen, ugly creature, and he lifted it up in his arms and hugged it, and called it by blusterous swear names, with noises of inarticulate affection. Then he went down to his berth in the second cabin and opened a little box of letters, and took them out one by one, and leaned up to the port to read them. He had read them before, and he knew them by heart, but he traced the lines with his broad forefinger, and spelled the words one by one. And as he did so he laughed aloud, and then cried to himself, and then laughed once more. "She is well and happy, and looking lovely, and, if she does not write, don't think she is forgetting you."

"God bless her. And God bless him, too. God bless them both!"

He went up on deck again, for he could not rest in one place long. There was a breeze now, and he filled his lungs and blew and blew. The island was dying down over the sea in a pale light of silver grey. An engineman and a stoker were leaning over the bulwark to cool themselves.

"Happy enough now, sir, eh?"

"Happy as a sand-boy, mate, only mortal hungry. Tiffin you say? Aw, the heart has its hunger same as anything else, and mine has been on short commons these five years and better. See that island there, lying like a salmon gull atop of the water? Looks as if she might dip under it, doesn't she? That's my home, my native land, as the man says, and only three weeks ago I wasn't looking to see the thundering ould thing again; but God is good, you see, and I am middling fit for all. I'm a Manxman myself, mate, and I've got a lil Manx woman that's waiting for me yonder. It's only an ould shirt I'm bringing her to patch, as the saying is, but she'll be that joyful you never seen. It's bad to take a woman by surprise, though—these nervous creatures—'sterics, you see—I'll send her a tally graph from the Stage. My sakes! the joy she'll be taking of that boy, too! He'll be getting sixpence for himself and a drink of butter-milk. It's always the way of these poor lil things—can't stand no good news at all—people coming home and the like—not much worth, these women—crying reglar—can't help it. Well, you see, they're tender-hearteder than us, and when anybody's been five years... Be gough, we're making way, though! The island's going under, for sure. Or is it my eyes that isn't so clear since my bit of a bullet-wound! Aw, God is good, tremen-jous!"

The breaking voice stopped suddenly, and the engine-men turned about, but the passenger was stumbling down the cabin stairs.

"If ever a man came back from the dead it's that one," said both men together.